Julep Street

Julep Street

CRAIG LANCASTER

MISSOURI BREAKS PRESS

The characters and events portrayed in this book are fictitious. Any similarity to real persons, living or dead, is coincidental and not intended by the author.

Published by Missouri Breaks Press, P.O. Box 50729, Billings, MT 59105

ISBN-10: 0982782241
ISBN-13: 978-0982782248

For Elisa. Always. Forever.

And with memories of every newspaper colleague I ever had.
To work with you was to be among the smartest,
funniest, most astute people I've ever known.
I wish you well, wherever you are.

The Far Side of Monday

Carson tells his dog about the day while opening a can of the salmon-and-rice formula that Hector prefers. Carson wrenches a fork under the punctured lid and plies it up, drops it into the plastic grocery bag on the cabinet knob, and then he describes the news as "a sledgehammer to the solar plexus." The pleasing lilt of the words gives him a flush of pride. A beat later comes the ache he has harbored since the email crawled to the top of his inbox. His ability with the quick turns of phrase, those nightly pieces of poetry in patterned picas, has underpinned not just his career but his manner of living.

"No more night owl," he tells Hector, who shifts his weight and licks his lips.

Carson moves through time on a schedule opposite that of regular folks, takes meals in restaurant booths with his back to the door and his eyes chasing down the newspaper and his mood hinging on whether he finds it in error. He delivers one a.m. feedings to his only true love, an expiring dog.

In his twenties, before Hector, Carson might have whiled

away the early morning hours at Shoney's, blowing off the steam from his shift by lobbing innuendo at Lurleen, who never responded with anything but forced toleration and the runny eggs he'd ordered.

"Have to figure out something else now," he says now to the dog. "For all of it."

The wet food falls into the bowl, and that's the signal for Hector to wobble onto arthritic legs and lurch from the living-room carpet to the chipped, yellowing linoleum. He drops his snout into the bowl. The dog has yielded everything to advancing time except his appetite, and that, Carson knows, is hastening his demise. In the past couple of years, as first running and then any sort of extended movement have betrayed the Lab, Hector's body has gone from sleek to distended and engorged.

Carson watches the dog eat and he thinks of Candy the ranch hand in his favorite Steinbeck book, and of the dog Candy kept too long. Carson kneels beside Hector and sets his ear on the dog's back, listening for a heartbeat that is smothered by gluttonous consumption.

"That's my boy," Carson says, threading his fingers against the grain of the short yellow hairs and feeling Hector's ribs through a layer of flab. Hector, a genial dog, sweeps his tail with a *swack, swack, swack* against the wall, and chomps down the last of the food. Carson keeps his head and hand in place, drumming on Hector's side, fingering the beat of that old Journey song as made-up lyrics slip out in a whisper.

Just a big ol' pup
He has trouble standin' up
But his bud Carson will take him anywhere
The news is shitty, boy
And I'm too broke to buy a toy
Let's hop a midnight train goin' anywhere...

Hector cranes his neck right and flops his tongue sideways,

and it connects with a clammy slap against Carson's right cheek.

"You don't like my singing?"

Swack, swack, swack.

"You do?"

Swack, swack, swack.

"OK, boy."

L ater, Carson lies awake, looking for patterns in the ceiling plaster through the mordant gray of early morning. Hector, a dog of grand delusion, moans from the foot of the bed, paws twitching, muscle memory giving chase to the rabbits that gather nightly in his head.

Carson's thoughts fall again on the email, now the polar north of his preoccupation. It arrived from Benny Haller with the subject line "re: great news!", and that, in the sad twang of hindsight, makes it all the harder for Carson to stomach.

> *Carson:*
>
> *I appreciate you taking the time to write yesterday. I shared it with my sister, and I hope what I have to say next doesn't cause you to regret any of the fine things you said about our family.*
>
> *We're coming to town tomorrow to tell folks this personally, but as you're the editor of the Argus-Dispatch I want you to know first: We're shutting the newspaper down. I don't have to tell you how untenable the financials of this business have become, and though as an isolated market we've been able to ride some of them out a little better than some other papers, the truth is the future isn't very bright. I suspect you know all of this. In the 13 years since we sold the paper and put it in the hands of a succession of public companies, you've seen what's happened.*

You're producing your own paper and two other community replates. Staffing has been slashed again and again. Ad lineage is down to nothing. I'll stop there. I'm not telling you anything you don't know.

But we're proud of the legacy in town and at the paper, and we're going to be seeding a fundraising drive to build a museum to Daddy there, where the archives and the press and some of the artifacts will be on permanent display, so future generations can appreciate what he built and what fine journalists like you sustained for so long.

I ask you to keep this to yourself and let us deliver the news tomorrow, along with some severance for the good people we'll be saying goodbye to. You've got two more editions to put out. Make them great.

All the best,
Benny Haller

The first of those two editions, the one Carson and his threadbare crew put to bed just a few hours ago, had been good enough for the way things are now but a damn sight removed from the days when Carson would walk the floor and say, "All right, gang, perfect-paper night" and mean it. Since Clemmons took the buyout last winter, Carson has had Dobber pulling triple duty covering city governments, none to what would have been considered a satisfying degree even a year before. When a fistfight broke out in the august offices of the Muhlenberg County commissioners, Dobber of course had been in McLean County, where the agenda had seemed more promising. The Muhlenberg punchout ran as a brief cobbled together from police reports and a quickie phone call from Carson to an old buddy on the council, not the wild yarn it could have been had Carson found a way to get a reporter there.

And it wasn't just that whiff, which was depressing enough. Molly begged off sick midway through her shift—her twenty-third such absence, a number Carson didn't have to look up—and so the weather page and the business briefs got jammed through in the final fifteen minutes of the shift, a turnaround so frantic that Carson scarcely remembers what was in them.

After everybody had cleared out for the night, Carson's flaccid thanks trailing them, he had slipped into the archives and pulled some old photos and story excerpts for the next day's final edition. He aimed to make it a full retrospective of the *Argus-Dispatch* and its past as a benevolent force for truth and civic advancement in the Ohio River Valley. As he dug into the clip files, he lingered on long-ago bylines of folks who had spun off to other papers and other places, and in some cases off the mortal coil. *The fortunate ones who won't have to see what's coming tomorrow.*

The unearthing brought forth forgotten artifacts. Here, the four-page wraparound section the day after Kentucky beat Syracuse for the 1996 NCAA title, a crowning nearly twenty years in the waiting for a fan base that had grown despondent at mediocrity. There, a 1988 picture of Benny Haller, a mammoth Canon hanging from his scrawny neck, as he played photojournalist. To old man Burton Haller's credit, he had demanded that his boy learn the business from the ground up, and in three years Benny had bounced from photo staff to reporter to ad rep to vice president, where he took wisdom at daddy's knee. A few years after the old man's death, Benny had sold the *Argus-Dispatch* to a big California media outlet for a reported thirty million dollars. All these years later, Carson still has trouble reconciling Benny Haller the young media baron with the deferential, nervous young man who lived across the hall from him in '88. Carson wonders how Benny will do tomorrow, when he faces the final few survivors of a dying newspaper and tells them their time is through. The folks who knew Benny back then are gone, except for Carson and a couple of others. Those people all liked Benny, because he was impossible not to like, but they also thought him slight compared with his father. They're not likely to be more charitable when Benny tells them they are obsolete. *Can he look them in the eye? Will he?* Carson blanches at being curious to find out.

He eases onto his side, careful not to rouse Hector, and returns his thoughts to the email. He's ashamed of the short message he had pecked out a day earlier, captured below Benny Haller's mournful reply.

> *Benny!*
> *Just heard that news that the family is back in the Argus-Dispatch business. It's not the least bit of puffery to say that this paper was never better than when your Dad was running it, and I look forward to a return to that excellence with you again at the publisher's helm. Can't wait!*
> *— C*

Hector shifts and whimpers, a signal not of dreamland rabbits but of recurrent arthritic pain. Carson sits up, tugging a T-shirt over his exposed belly roll, and stretches his arms out, finding the dog's head. He slips his index finger behind Hector's ear and digs deep, and the Lab exhales like a lawnmower on the first tug of spring.

Carson lies back, the girth rolls forth, and again he pulls his shirt down. *Don't have money. Got lots of time. Exercise is overdue.*

He closes his eyes and squeezes them tight, bringing on a field of black. It doesn't take long. Exhaustion wins again, and Carson's own dreamy haze settles onto his fraying brain, white letters on a billboard crawl: *We're shutting the newspaper down. We're shutting the newspaper down. We're shutting the newspaper down.*

Tuesday Morning

Same shit, different day. Carson stands outside the apartment in the chill at 6:03, *rat-a-tat-tatting* his right foot as Hector gives glancing consideration to the only five trees he knows, at last lifting his leg on the blue ash that always gets christened. The rest goes by rote, too. Hector walks a few tentative steps, lifts his nose to consider the aroma of the morning, then squats, hind legs quaking, until he ejects a titanic turd. Hector resets himself, stands with whatever dignity he can muster, and barks.

"Good boy," Carson says. He strides over and sweeps the load into the reversed-out yellow newspaper bag that covers his hand (*going to have to steal a bunch of them before I turn over my key*), and already Hector makes his way up the stairs like a Slinky in reverse, the front paws finding purchase and the hindquarters flopping up behind.

Later, Hector's nose is in a fresh bowl of food and Carson stands at the bathroom mirror, for the first time in his working life uncertain of what to wear. Any other day—*every* other day—it would be the khakis and the white button-front shirts he keeps in boxes, rotating them through wearings and dry cleanings. Today, he wonders if he should go with the plain black slacks he hasn't worn since last year's press association dinner. Maybe a tie, too. Something subdued and appropriate for the regrettable occasion. He worries that someone will see the change in attire and deduce that something bad is coming down, and that's that. He wriggles into the khakis and the usual white shirt and figures that if the new-boss-soon-to-be-the-old-boss thinks it too casual, well, what's the worst that can happen?

At 6:24, Hector nestles into his spot on the bed, and Carson flips to the classic-movie channel that occupies the dog's day. Carson then slides out the door, six minutes ahead of schedule.

The boulevard shimmers in the early light, and Carson decides that the knotted tangle in his stomach isn't all that different from any other day's. Exactly twenty-four hours earlier—his six-minute cushion is gone, thanks to a stop for two dozen sorry-you-don't-have-a-job-anymore doughnuts— he drove this route and worried that this would be the time the *Argus-Dispatch* wouldn't be produced, that all the paring that had long since cut through staffing flab into sinew and bone would take its toll, that the night desk of two would be one (after Molly called in sick) and then none (after Carson said "screw it" and went home to Hector) and folks in town would wake up and find their driveways bare.

Carson laughs, bitter and contemptuous, at the realization that his paranoia was off by just a day.

He turns right off Julep Street, into the parking lot of the low-slung concrete bunker that dominates a city block. Carson remembers how different this all was when he arrived with a freshly calligraphed B.A. from Murray State in 1986. Then, the *Argus-Dispatch* building struck him more as bucolic campus than foreboding workplace. It was ringed by a fulsome lawn (now ceded to garden stones, all the better to not employ a landscaping crew), with a fountain in front (torn out and cemented over eight years ago) and an interior flow that, east to west, allowed for easy passage through the chronological order of producing a daily newspaper: front desk, business office, ad sales, ad layout, newsroom, composing room, camera room, press.

Carson pushes himself out of his Tercel—bought in '93 on a four-year note, when a paycheck from the *Argus-Dispatch* impressed lenders with the patina of reliability—and walks toward what now looks more like a downmarket strip mall. For three years, Mantooth Media has been leasing out chunks of the building, and now when Carson walks from the newsroom to the press he must pass a spray-tan salon (Janz Tanz), a small-engine-repair place ("Red's Will Get You Revvin' Again"), and a party supply store (Bombastic Balloons and Bashes). He learned the hard way that the balkanization of the office posed security challenges.

Last June, the night desk went to dinner together and came back to find two Mac design terminals gone. Nothing could be proved, but circumstances and word on the street suggested that Red has a nice side job of fencing stolen goods. Since then, the company mandated that someone stay in the office at all times during evening production hours—expedient policy that had the attendant effect of further eroding the night crew's camaraderie.

At the front door, Carson turns back, dipping his right shoulder to keep the doughnut boxes in balance, and looks at the parking lot. The Tercel sits next to a glimmering Lexus that can belong only to Benny Haller, and in Carson's off-kilter sense of humor the cars morph into the yappy mutt and the muscular bulldog from the old Warner Bros. cartoon.

How about we go inside and thrash a newspaper, Alfie old boy? How'd you like that?

Blimey, lad, did you say newspaper? Lead on.

The acid rises in Carson's throat. He chokes it down.

He sets his weight into the glass door, and it swings open.

B enny Haller sweeps his monogrammed left cuff with the back of his right hand, irritated by the atmospheric dust. "Tell me about your crew," he says.

Carson puts his arms on the rests of the chair that fronts his commandeered desk and shifts his weight from his right butt cheek to his left.

"What do you want to know?"

Benny stands and walks past him to the doorway and looks across the empty newsroom, as Carson turns the chair in sputters. "I mean, tell me their names, a little history. I don't want to be a hatchet man here. I want them to know I appreciate what they've done."

"Keep the paper going then." The words muscle out of Carson's mouth, the last syllable hanging in the air as he realizes the impudence of it.

Haller turns to him. *It's the same guy I knew*, Carson thinks. *A bloated version—a lot of that going around—but the same face, the same head of hair, no gray that I can see. The bastard.* Minutes earlier, their first handshake in thirteen years had been friendly enough, but there was no mistaking that they sat on opposite sides of this thing—Haller about to deliver bad news to people Carson cares about, Carson holding pastries in a palliative gesture that now feels silly and impotent.

"Believe it or not, rebuilding the paper was what I had in mind when we first started sniffing around." Haller turns again to the open door, his back to Carson, and his words take on an angry edge. "I mean, Jesus, look what they've done to it. But when I realized what we could get it for, and what little it brings in, well, I just couldn't see my way clear to keeping it going. So we came up with another idea."

"What *did* you get it for?"

Benny drops back to the desk and sits in Carson's chair. "Proprietary information, my friend. But I'll say this: You might could have swung it with what's in your 401(k)."

"You severely overestimate my 401(k). Especially after today." Carson leaves it acidly at that as he remembers the number he looked up online at the end of trading yesterday, an act that has become compulsion in the past couple of years: $75,872.18. It's a paltry number measured against how many years Carson has put in and how many he figures he has left. He always thought he had more time, a good fifteen years at least before he was done here. He looks at his watch. 7:58 a.m. *Fifteen hours.*

Benny sits forward, fingers laced across the desk calendar that says January 2012, and Carson realizes he's three months behind. "Let's talk about that," Benny says.

"About what?"

"About 'especially after today.'"

Carson looks past Haller, to the wall behind his head. "OK, go ahead."

"But first, tell me about your people."

Carson empties the roster. He starts with the three Benny would remember—or who would remember him. Dub Dobber, who knows the secret ingredients of municipal sausage-making and has been manic on the job since his wife, Glennda, died of uterine cancer last spring. Herman Drumley, the photo chief who had to be hauled into the digital era by threat of losing his job. Boone Behrens, the sports editor, who has never forgiven Carson for posting one of his columns on the bulletin board some years back and writing over the headline, in red ink, "18 inches, 18 clichès," each one circled. (Carson later conceded to Dobber, over many rounds at the Cheerio, that it had been "a dick move." He just can't bring himself to say the same thing to Behrens, and now it doesn't much matter. When daily production feels more like excreting blood than craftsmanship, who can worry about something as inconsequential as clichè?)

That leaves the relative newbies: Timmy Bardo, the twenty-three-year-old sports reporter Carson hired in the fall. Molly Vernon, the human petri dish of illness. Burt Tomison, the cops reporter who sleeps with a police scanner. Jim Jolly, the crackerjack desk man. Elizabeth Blum, the other photographer. Holly Raymont, general-assignment reporter.

"And me," Carson says. "That's ten. When you sold the place, we had thirty-five in the newsroom."

Haller, he sees, has developed a good poker face. Twenty-five years ago, Benny couldn't find his socks half the time. Now he looks at Carson and betrays no hint of what he's thinking.

"How do you manage?" Haller asks.

"Not very well."

"No, seriously."

"Well." Carson exhales, long and loud, and shifts again in the chair. "Mostly, we figured out what to give up. Most of the weekly specialty sections are gone. No more technology. No more Saturday features. Health? Gone. We consolidated beats as we lost folks, either by attrition or layoffs. Dobber's covering every city and county government in our circulation area. We don't go to high school games unless it's something big—we just have our guys in the office, taking phone calls from coaches. That sort of thing. You've seen the paper. It's about half the size it was when you were here. Ads are scant. Costs twice as much, too, ads and the paper out of the box. More for less, only not in the way that Mantooth Media uses—*used*—the phrase."

"And what about you?"

"Me?" Carson laughs again, but he's looking away, unwilling to meet Haller's gaze. "Well, I'm here six days a week, early morning to midnight. I slip away for a couple of hours midday. On Sundays, I sleep. I'm scared to take a vacation. It's quite a life."

Haller leans forward. "There's gotta be something easier, don't you think?"

Carson looks down and pretends to pull a thread from his own cuff. "Yeah, but I figure unemployment has its own set of troubles. I guess I'm about to find out for sure."

"I've got a different idea," Haller says.

Haller starts by revealing what he has in mind today. Buildingwide, he'll tell fifty-two people there won't be work tomorrow, or any other day. He plans to soften the blow by handing out severance packages: two weeks' pay for every year someone has worked at the *Argus-Dispatch*, with a minimum of ten weeks and no maximum. Six months' health benefits, paid. Three free sessions with a career counselor and an employment placement specialist. Haller, on his way to make deliveries to the other managers, hands the newsroom packages to Carson and asks him to doublecheck the figures, and Carson sees that each folder has an employee's name stenciled on the cover, meaning Benny Haller didn't need to hear anything about the crew. He had the names and numbers straight along.

Everything pencils out, including Carson's package. Twenty-six years of service means fifty-two weeks' pay, and there it is, a year's earnings in a single check, minus taxes: $40,216.28.

In Haller's absence, Carson reclaims his chair and desk, and he rocks back, hands cupped behind his head, and for the first time feels as if he's breathing. The ten checks he holds alleviate a lot of the immediate concerns he's harboring, for himself and for his people. Some will have it tougher than others. He worries, in particular, about Timmy Bardo and hopes he can find something else before his ten weeks' dough runs dry. Blum and Raymont have husbands with good jobs, which grants Carson a peace of mind he wouldn't dare sound out to either of them. Molly will be in a bit of a bind, and Carson has already decided that he won't give her anything more than a tepid endorsement in light of her rampant absenteeism. The rest of them—Behrens, Dobber, Tomison, Drumley, Jolly—are close enough to retirement that the combination of the check and their savings might make it worth the stretch. In any case, Carson figures, he won't have to worry about them, but damn, it will be weird from now on to see these people at the grocery store and know they won't convene at the *Argus-Dispatch* later on.

Haller comes back in. "Everything look OK?"

Carson, caught in his wandering thoughts, scrambles back to the present. "Yeah, great," he says, snapping upright in the chair. "I have to say, Benny, this is really ... well, it's just a hell of a sporting thing you're doing, taking care of these folks this way. I didn't expect it. I mean, aw, hell, I was worried about it. Thanks. Truly, thanks."

Haller shuts the door. He sits down across the desk from Carson.

"It was beyond the right thing to do," he says. "It's a hell of a thing, to have your job just up and disappear, in this economic climate especially. But, look, there was some selfishness involved, too."

"How so?"

Haller tips his head forward and puts his hands on the desk and looks directly at Carson. The unease that has been gnawing at Carson all morning, the one that transcends this bloodless thing they're about to do, at last has clarity. This man across from him, whom he knew in another lifetime as a boy who'd just skated over to adulthood, has been locked in since Carson arrived, and no doubt long before that. He knew the questions, and the answers, before Carson even considered what they might be. Had Carson arrived in full bluster, squawking out a case for the cultural and democratic need of journalism, an *it's-bigger-than-we-are* screed, a *goddammit-you-just-can't-do-this* plea, Haller would have simply batted it all aside, lined everybody up, handed out his stenciled folders and retired to the Woodwind Cafè for a Cobb salad, the scattered lives on Julep Street but a hiccup in his day.

Damn, Carson thinks, *I gave this guy his first condom.*

"That's the part I want to talk to you about," Haller says. "We're going to build a museum that celebrates Dad right here in town, and to do that we need enthusiasm and, especially, donations from the community. If I blow in here and cut a bunch of people loose with no safety net, how's that gonna work out for us? Not good."

Carson wishes he had worn the tie. Haller has a nice one on. Purple, with chromatic, thin purple stripes. *How much would a tie like that cost?*

"Tell me how I can help," Carson says.

Haller is almost on top of the desk now, it seems. "First, stand with me today as we thank these men and women for their work. Then, put out the best fucking final edition you can. Go home. Relax. Take that check there. Sock it away, or put a down payment on a house, or whatever. Take a couple of weeks off while I get some people in here to box everything up for the move to the museum. Then be back here ready to help us raise the money for this thing as our executive director."

Carson imagines himself in another cartoon now, his tongue unfurled across the desk, out the door and down the hallway like a garden hose.

"Executive director? Benny, I don't—"

"Look, Carson, don't answer now. It's a lot to absorb. Take

a couple of weeks and think about it. I'm confident you'll be joining us. Nobody loved this place the way you did, and nobody is better qualified to tell the story of the Hallers and the *Argus-Dispatch* than you are."

Carson sits, numb. Haller looks at his watch.

"Almost 8:30," he says, standing up. "Let's do this."

Tuesday Night

The imagesetter strobes flash, painting the walls with amorphous, spinning yellow polka dots that herald the imminent arrival of the aluminum plates. Carson turns and counts heads. He comes up with twenty-nine, including Benny Haller's, right next to him. Molly and Jim are here, as usual, as are Dobber and Timmy Bardo, also regulars at this time of night.

The rest are welcome interlopers—ad reps and delivery drivers and business office folks, people who got up in the middle of the night and came back to the *Argus-Dispatch* one last time, to see the final pages onto the press.

Carson puts his attention back on the imagesetter as the wheels grind, pulling the plate through. A faint chemical odor sashays through the air.

"This is it," he calls out. "Front page. Last page." He holds his breath.

Haller, jacket discarded hours earlier, purple tie off, slips an arm behind Carson's neck and claps him on the shoulder.

He's been amazing to watch, Carson thinks. *Remembered every name. Made them all seem to accept—no, even appreciate— what he came here to do.* And then, lest Carson drift too far into admiration of this old chum, a crueler thought comes: *The daddy Haller so reveres seemed born to run this place. His boy, it turns out, was born to shut it down.*

The plate peeks out of the developer, and the top of the Old English "A" in *Argus-Dispatch* sets off spontaneous applause from the gathering. The plate pushes out of the developer, a birth in slow motion, and the group pushes forward for a look.

The page reveals itself in stages. The nameplate, its style little changed in one hundred and ten years. Below that, a reversed-out gray bar: "The News Source of The Ohio River Valley." And then, finally, comes the headline, all-caps, two decks at 120 points, centered:

IT WAS
OUR PLEASURE

The stories on the page move forward and backward through time. In a publisher's note that was written by hand on a yellow legal pad and handed to Carson for typing into the computer system, Haller makes his case for closure, "economic environment" being an especially useful all-purpose euphemism, and for a curated future celebrating the history of a newspaper and dead-in-the-ground Burton Haller and his daddy before him. The thirty-two-page, single-section edition brims with nostalgia, a thrown-together retrospective of a town and its newspaper. To its dying day, the *Argus-Dispatch* excelled at putting history into context. Making sense of the future would fall on other shoulders, Benny Haller wrote. It was this realization, which Carson reached on his own three hours earlier as he walked a page proof from the printer back to the desk, that finally sent him to his knees in the men's room. He surprised himself by crying, just for a moment, for the loss. He grew up here, graduated from high school here, and once a year went to the same church he'd known as a boy, a nod to the parents now gone who always wished he'd found more guidance there. He had never contemplated that the city or the newspaper could survive without each other, so entwined were their histories. To be so spectacularly wrong about that made him wonder what else he'd missed these past twenty-six years, which set off another crying jag, one Carson stopped by replacing it with rage and tearing the paper towel dispenser out of the wall.

The group leans in as the plate goes through the bender and into Larry Pierson's hands. The old pressman carries it through the door that stands sentry between the imagesetter room and the press, and in that instant the oily stench of ink blasts through the open door and into the faces of the gathering. The simple act inspires instant, crushing nostalgia, and Carson's mind drifts away again. When he came here, cold type galleys still spat out of massive, boxy developers. Those were cut to long ribbons by exacto-knife-wielding production crews who built pages to specifications sketched out onto layout sheets by the desk editors. Now, in minutes, the pages go from computer screen to pressmen's waiting hands. For one more night, anyway.

As the crew watches through portal windows, Pierson hangs the plate on the cylindrical drum and then drops back to the control panel. A pushed button brings a short burst of an alarm. The other two pressmen on duty give a thumbs-up. Pierson punches a few more buttons and the cylinders turn. He gooses the press, and it speeds up, the smudgy first few papers yielding to clearer, sharper images, until finally, Pierson sees what he wants, a precise rendering of the front page. The press is at cruising speed now.

Carson looks over his shoulder. Nobody's smiling. No clapping. No cheering. A few hold each other. A few dab at their eyes. All of them know, if they didn't know before. This is it.

Carson walks to the press room door and accepts a bundle of papers from Pierson, and he hands them out. People take them, but except for Haller, nobody seems eager about it. They accept the newsprint with tentative hands and downcast eyes.

It's all over but the dying.

C arson sweeps crumbs off the desk into the doughnut box. "Leave it," Haller says. "Cleanup crew will be here day after tomorrow."

Carson finishes the job, crumples the box and stashes it in the garbage can at his feet. It's been an hour since the press run ended, and already the place looks abandoned. The night crew, with banker's boxes supplied by Haller, packed up their belongings and headed home. Carson held the front door open for them, offering handshakes and hugs to those who wanted them, and a promise to get together soon that he knew was a lie even as it slipped off his tongue.

"You want my key?" he says to Haller.

"Keep it. You'll be back."

Carson's head feels as if it's unraveling, a sensation that is equal parts sleep deprivation (ongoing), stress (ditto) and bewilderment (a new development). "Benny, I don't know."

"Hold your water," Haller says, rapping his knuckles on the Formica. "Take a few days before you say that. It's an emotional time. Keep your key. Come back in a couple of weeks."

"You don't seem emotional," Carson says. "You seem like you're enjoying this."

Just for an instant, Carson thinks he sees a threatening storm on the periphery of Haller's face, and then it's gone, tamped down by rehearsed, refined CEO comportment.

"Did you cry today?" Haller asks.

The question catches Carson leaning the wrong way, but he knows Haller already has the answer. They had met eyes after Carson left the men's room, and the sniffles had been impossible to hide. "Yes," Carson says.

Haller retrieves his tie from the desk and hangs it across his shoulders. "Don't mistake a sense of opportunity for a lack of caring. Today, I'm focused on what's to come. Yesterday, *I* cried."

Wednesday, Early

C arson sits up and blinks into the darkness to find his bearings. The clock on the end table flashes 5:03 in red LED, and Carson stretches across himself to flip the alarm button off. The corresponding red dot on the display fades out.

Hector, ensconced in a black-and-white dream, lies across the covers and atop his master's feet. Carson extricates them slowly, careful not to wake the dog, and hears the scratch of his heels against the sheet. He rolls toward the far side of the bed, away from the clock, arms and legs akimbo, and finds the floor. Hector yawns—a long, distressed yawp—and Carson reaches behind the dog's ear and massages deeply, sending his boy back into contented slumber.

T he emails have been gathering and multiplying overnight, a mèlange of messages from old friends, former co-workers, astonished industry professionals, and a few hateful ax-grinders. The media writer at *The New York Times* wants to talk as soon as possible "about the extraordinary act of killing off a small-town newspaper, the kind that was supposed to be best-positioned to emerge from publishing dystopia." An economics professor at Western Kentucky wants a chronology of the final day, with the hope that he can build it into a lesson plan about disruptive technology's role in a vibrant economy. To this, Carson types a reply—"Fuck you"—that he saves as a draft. John Hume, who started at the *Argus-Dispatch* on the same June day in 1986 as Carson, sends his regrets from the P.R. office of the Dallas Cowboys. Madelyn in Rosine wants Carson to know that the leftist bias of the paper finally did it in, and not a moment too soon. His mother's shirttail cousin, the mayor of Grandview, Montana, wants to know if he wants a job. *Yeah, Montana. No, thanks.* A few messages come with nothing more than "WTF?" in the subject line.

Carson is halfway through a response to the *Times* reporter, lost in a tangle of tangents and burning through hundreds of words in a flailing effort at identifying where it all went wrong. The slow erosion of the *Argus-Dispatch* wasn't linear, and the pieces don't all fit together, even in the cold light of morning and unemployment. How do you identify the source of a collapse when the bricks have been removed one at a time over the decades? Carson thinks back to 1999, when they got the technology to send pages directly from the desktop to film. The four guys in the composing room were escorted out in short order, their X-Acto knives and their full-time salaries no longer necessary to the operation. Carson would see Mel Hardricker or Jon Leek around from time to time, at Skinny's or maybe the Cheerio, and it was as if they couldn't look at each other for long or speak in unstilted ways, like how they used to on the loading dock during breaks. Too much resentment, and too much attendant survivor's guilt. Benny Haller had plowed some of that savings back into the newspaper: a new technology section, and an extra sports reporter. How could Carson face those guys knowing that their ouster made his job better? Now, of course, it's a moot point. Haller sold the paper a year later, and soon enough, the technology section was gone and so was the bonus reporter. Every quarter, a chunk of what remained got lopped off—advertising art outsourced to India, the reporting staff shaved off a beat at a time, lower-watt bulbs popped into the light fixtures—until Benny walked back in and fired the final, fatal shot.

Carson looks at the scattershot of words across his screen. They're incoherent and strident, and they'll do him no good. His left thumb and forefinger find CTRL-A, and he flicks at the delete button with his right pinkie. The message goes away, and then he replaces it.

> *I have no comment. Recommend you direct all inquiries to Benny Haller.*

He hits send before he can reconsider, and it's gone.

The other emails, a stack that grows by a message or two a minute, he answers with a single word: "Thanks." The last one parried, at least for now, he turns the computer off before more regards come through.

Carson lies down on the bed, his feet at the headboard, his face on the back of Hector's neck. He sets his head on his own right shoulder and dangles his arm off the bed. His left arm curls across Hector's ribs, his hand cupping the dog's breastbone. Hector speaks in a manner, his own somnambulant language, and then he noses Carson's hand, licking the spaces between the fingers and then falling back into deep snore-sighs.

It's 6:37. Carson closes his eyes.

Wednesday, Mid-Afternoon

Hector noses the long grass at the base of the trees, distracted. Carson stands in his usual spot, still in a T-shirt and pajama bottoms, and wedges his right hand against his forehead to hold back the sun. Hunger gnaws at his gut.

Hector slides his snoot along the ground and dips his head, and the rest of his body follows. He rolls onto his back and wriggles atop a dead bird.

"No!"

Hector keeps flopping, until Carson stamps his foot and threatens to come at him. "Come on, boy." Animal instinct overrides what Hector must know by now, that Carson would never raise a hand to him. Hector stands, as quickly as he can, and lurches back toward the trees. He lifts a hind leg, and the rest of his pegs quiver in the whizzing. He settles back onto all-fours and drops anchor, and he deposits fertilizer.

"Good boy."

C arson puts food in Hector's dish and presents it. The dog cocks his head.

"Yeah, I know, it's not the usual time. We were asleep, remember?"

Hector blinks.

"Eat. It's OK."

Hector looks at the food.

"Eat!"

Hector at last accedes.

Carson digs through the refrigerator. Chinese takeout he should have tossed a week ago. A half-empty bottle of green salsa. A couple of slices of cheese and some margarine. He unwinds the twist tie from the bread bag and pulls out two slices of white. One at a time, he holds them to the light and turns them. The first slice passes examination. The second one he sets on the countertop and pinches at the crust, excising a bit of mold. He examines it again.

T he sandwich toasts in the frying pan, and Carson flips on the radio. On workday mornings, he would catch up on the overnight news, making notes about what his staff will need to chase but mostly listening as the voice reads, verbatim, what is in the *Argus-Dispatch*. Today, at this hour, there is no news, only the braying voice of Barry Bowersox. Carson turns the volume down a notch.

"Good people, we've been talking about it for years, and at last it has come to pass. The *Argus-Dispatch* is no more, consigned to the dustbin of history and soon to be a museum piece, a proper resting place for an obsolete media form. But I didn't come here to bury the *Argus-Dispatch*. I'm here to mourn what it could have been, rather than what it was: a tool of the socialistic interests in this country that would rather enslave us than allow us to live in liberty."

Carson lifts the sandwich onto his plate with the spatula and then cuts it diagonally. The melted cheese oozes into the resulting gap.

"Did you read Benny Haller's note on the front page today, friends? I like Benny, I really do, but what a bunch of bull that was. The *Argus-Dispatch* didn't die because of a bad economy or a lack of revenue. There's no better capitalist in this state than Benny Haller—the guy's hands are in everything. He could have made the newspaper back into the giant it once was, but give him credit. He recognized that the paper had poisoned itself with its biases. Credit to him for realizing that and taking it out back and shooting it like you would a hobbled dog."

Carson, wincing, sits next to Hector at the foot of the bed.

"When did we ever see success stories in the *Argus-Dispatch*? Never. We saw stories about poor people and failing charities and health care. Trumped-up stories to rile the self-disenfranchised minority. The *Argus-Dispatch* was invested in the misery of this place, not in its promise, not in its achievements. How many Republican candidates has the *Argus-Dispatch* ever endorsed? I'll tell you the answer, good people: zero. But it never saw a government program it wouldn't praise or a spending initiative that it wouldn't embrace. Let's face it, folks. The *Argus-Dispatch* needed to die so the rest of us could live free. Call us at 794-1978 if you want to talk about this."

One bite taken, Carson sets the sandwich on the desk. He's up and headed for the telephone, the landline he's had since he took the job at the paper, the one that became passè a dozen years ago and now makes him the object of gentle derision from co-workers (former co-workers) and the occasional date (*very* occasional date).

Carson's right hand holds the phone under the cradle, and with his left he punches the numbers.

On the other end, a ring.

"This guy's a joke," Carson says to Hector. The dog regards him idly.

Another ring.

"Come on."

The line engages. "You're on with Barry Bowersox. What's your beef?"

Carson's plan for what to say, only half-concocted when he picked up the phone and dialed, drops out of his head at his sudden emergence on live air, and he scrambles to find words.

"I think—" Angular and metallic, the feedback crashes out of the radio speakers. Hector's ears perk, and he whines at Carson.

"Turn off your radio, friend," Bowersox says, and Carson scoots across the studio apartment and shuts it down.

"Better?" he asks.

"Go ahead, friend."

"Anyway, as I was saying, I think you don't have a clue what you're talking about."

Bowersox, an old hand at such challenges, chuckles—a smirky *heh-heh-heh*—and says, "Well, that's not exactly an original contention. Show your work."

"Well, to start with, let's talk economy." Carson paces back and forth in front of the bed, a toy soldier on patrol. Hector's head bobs along. "You blithely dismiss the economics of the thing, but the truth is, every newspaper—not just this one—is seeing advertising dollars march right out the door. You picked up a paper lately? It's a damn pamphlet."

"But there's still an audience, my friend. That's what I hear from the *Argus-Dispatch* all the time: 'Our audience is bigger than ever. Thanks to the Internet, we're read more than ever.' You telling me there's no money for the *Argus-Dispatch*? When I have a big audience—and believe you me, friend, I do—I make money hand over fist."

"Ah, yeah, the Internet," Carson says. "Did you know that, nationwide, newspapers are losing seven print advertising dollars for every one dollar in Internet revenue that comes in. That's not a downward trend, man. That's a king-size commode flushing." Carson comes to a full stop, waiting.

"What's your name, friend?" Bowersox says. Carson imagines the radio jock's eyes narrowing on the other end of the line. "You sound like you're in the know on this deal."

Carson slips the phone into his left hand and pats Hector on the head with his right. "Call me the Barry Bowersox Truth Squad."

"Heh-heh-heh. All right, friend. Have it your way."

"So let's talk about this political nonsense you're spewing." Carson is back on patrol, with faster sweeps across the room. "You say the paper doesn't endorse Republican candidates."

"It doesn't."

"You're wrong. In the last election, out of eighteen competitive races, the paper endorsed the Republican candidate in nine of them." Carson knows this neatly cleaved number because editorial marching orders from Mantooth Media dictated an even split, whenever possible, in party endorsements, so as not to alienate readers from either party—or, rather, to alienate them in equal numbers. If Barry Bowersox wants true dirt on the *Argus-Dispatch* agenda, there it is.

"Interesting," Bowersox says. "Of course, we'll have to verify that, but in any case, I was making a larger point—"

"Yeah, yeah, you were making a larger point, but that point is bogus, too, and you make it with lies and disinformation."

"Friend—"

"Shut up, Bowersox. You say the paper never highlights stories of achievement, which is a lie right there, but let me ask you something: Where's all this achievement in a business and economic sense? Downtown's mostly boarded up. We've got more kids born into poverty in this town than ever before because most of the good jobs are gone. My old man worked at the aluminum plant, and I give thanks every day that he didn't live to see that go away. The Super Valu Saver Store was a hell of an achievement. It achieved the goal of shutting down damn near every locally owned retailer in town. It's hollowed out the core of this town so it can stand out there on the highway and draw us all in with low, low prices—"

"People like low, low prices."

"Yeah, they do. But don't you see what we've lost? Let's go back to newspaper advertising. Klein's Meat Market advertised in the *Argus-Dispatch*, but it's been gone eight years because people would rather get their steak at Super Valu Saver. The IGA sponsored the American Legion team. It pulled out last year, and now there's another empty storefront on Julep Street, and we've got young ballplayers selling their mommas' apple pies so they can buy socks. We used to have three tire stores in this town, all competitive, all advertisers. They're gone because Super Valu Saver can put the tires on while you buy your groceries. And Super Valu Saver doesn't advertise in the *Argus-Dispatch*. It doesn't have to. We flock to it because we have no other choice."

"You seem to have a problem with convenience, friend."

"No, I have a problem with eating our own prosperity so we can save nineteen cents on a bottle of shampoo." Carson is shouting. Hector slides off the bed and hobbles into the closet. "I have a problem with actively working to undermine our own self-interest. You think Super Valu Saver is convenient? Yeah, I guess so, if you can ignore all the unseen ways its hands are in your pocket. You like to rail about how government is robbing you blind. Well, Super Valu Saver has robbed us all of economic liberty, of the opportunity to shop where we want, to support our neighbors who are in business, of our tax base. Certain things, if you want them in this town, you have to go to Super Valu Saver. It has made us captives. Where's your outrage about that?"

"Heh heh heh."

"Finally, Bowersox, I have a big problem with people like you making your bones by stoking the mouth-breathers against a newspaper that was on their side. You're real good at concocting enemies, making people fearful of them, and advancing your own agenda. And you don't give a damn about helping people. Now that the newspaper is gone, who's going to tell folks when something really threatens them, like the superintendent siphoning off tax dollars for his personal use? You, Bowersox? That's a laugh."

Carson finishes. His heart flip-flops in his chest, and the sweat slides sideways across the top of his forehead. Hector is up, peeking around the corner to see if it's safe to venture back into the main room.

Barry Bowersox waits out a dramatic beat of empty air, milking it, letting Carson's words linger. "The phone lines just lit up like a bonfire," he says at last. "Heh-heh-heh. 'Mouth-breathers,' friend? Well, this has been fun, but it's time for Uncle Barry to move on to another call after this commercial break. And friend, you better hope none of these people know your name."

The line goes dead in Carson's hands. He drops the phone to the floor, the ringer clanging as it strikes tile. Carson picks up his sandwich, goes to the kitchen, and throws it away.

The question of Carson's identity, he decides in the car, is uncomfortably obscure. The first subsequent caller has him pegged: "That's Carson McCullough, sure enough. He came and spoke to my Rotary club one time, so I know the voice. Talking about our duty to each other and other socialistic bullroar. And you hear the way he talked about people who listen to your show, Barry? Why, that's the kind of arrogance that the *Argus-Dispatch* has been displaying for years, and I for one am glad to see it exterminated."

But the next two callers insist that it's not Carson, that they know him and can vouch that he's a respectable local boy who'd never be so categorically impolite. (Carson is mesmerized by this, wondering who these generous souls are who think so much of him, as he's flat unable to even conjure a fuzzy image from the voices.) One talks of outside agitators coming into the community to stir up trouble and maybe this talkative fellow on the radio is one of those America haters. The other surmises that the mystery guest was Benny Haller himself, a contention that Bowersox smothers. "Benny Haller's one of my best friends," he says, and Carson plows a fist into the console, cracking the frame of an air conditioning vent and peeling back the skin of his middle knuckle like the pop top on a yogurt container. He puts the knuckle in his mouth and slurps the blood that tastes like old pennies.

Carson cuts to the back aisles of Super Valu Saver, away from the knots of shoppers, and paranoia sinks in. Each look that lingers a second too long, he's convinced, belongs to someone who has connected him to the Bowersox show. One woman, in faded pink sweat pants a size too small and with two fat, crusty-mouthed boys, regards him with open contempt, and he slides to his right and sweeps his arm with generosity to let her pass. She does so but holds the stare until she's halfway down the aisle and unable to crane her neck further. Carson stands still. He watches her reach the end of the line and turn right, toward home electronics. He looks down, and there's the answer. He looks left and right and is alone, and he pulls his belly roll in with his left hand. The fly on his jeans is open, disregarded in his haste to get out of the apartment.

The flaps are turned out, and his flaccid dingus is there for anyone to see.

Another plush chew toy that Hector will destroy by the weekend. A gallon of milk. A loaf of fresh bread. Peanut butter. Deodorant. Carson holds the items in tentative balance and goose-steps to the bank of registers. The tally comes to $21.43, and Carson fishes out his bank card to pay. He reminds himself to go to the bank today and deposit the severance. This purchase will be scraping at the bottom of his checking account.

On cue, the cashier turns on her corporate smile, looks through Carson and wishes him a good day. He heads for the automatic door. Each hand holds a plastic bag, and he walks sideways like a crab, the paperback he swiped riding low in the ass of his jeans.

Wednesday, Late Night

The years have not been merciful to Lurleen. Carson sits in a booth and peeks over his book, watching her. *What's it been now, five years? Seven? Ten?* He has an inkling of a late-night dinner here not so long ago, but then he thinks it over and decides it might have been at Skinny's on the west end. *Who was there? Somebody up from Paducah? Some Mantooth suit?* Clarity can't penetrate the half-constructed memory, and Carson lets it go. In any case, it's been a good piece since he's seen Lurleen, and the greasy-spoon goddess of his fantasies has vacated the stage for this gone-gray, portly, middle-aged woman who grinds down her shoes on the outside edges.

Lurleen moves along the periphery with a pot of coffee, caffeinated salvation for the other people scattered about the place. On a pass by the kitchen, she swoops in for a slice of lemon meringue and sets it in front of the wiry-haired codger sitting along the east window. She's more tanker than dinghy these days, Lureen is, but Carson gives credit. She still glides.

She sidles up to the table. "What'll it be?"

Carson sets his book down, splayed out to hold his place. "It's been a long time, Lurleen."

"It has?"

"You don't remember me?" The words are quick and shrill, too much so in each case, and Carson wishes he could have them back.

"Not especially."

"No? I used to come in here a lot." He tries to hide the hurt—the stupid, inexplicable hurt. "You know, I'd toss innuendo at you, and you'd tell me to pound sand. We were friendly that way."

She shifts her weight from her left foot to her right and shakes the order book at him. "Look, sweetie, it ain't exactly an exclusive group that chats up Lurleen, or gets told to pound sand." It's not lost on Carson that the third person that would otherwise repel him—*this reporter finds such affectation to be silly*—in this instance enchants him with its random verve.

"I guess not," he says. "Two eggs over easy, hashbrowns, bacon." She jots the order, takes the menu and heads back to her rounds. Carson watches the wiggle as she goes.

Carson picks up the book again. The main character, an author whose manuscript has just sold, is being extorted by the ex-con husband of the woman he's shagging on the side. He's now explaining to the con that he doesn't have $100,000 to give him, that the money's coming in three installments over the next two years and that, furthermore, paying four years in back taxes has pretty well erased the first infusion. This is not sitting well, and gunplay seems a distinct possibility.

Carson remains on the surface of the words, his mind hours back at Super Valu Saver, in the bookshelves, where he waited for the area to clear of customers, grabbed the book without looking at it, and shoved it down the back of his pants. Later, at the apartment, he told Hector that it was like coming alive—equal measures of terror and exhilaration as he walked to the cash register. Interpreting the face of the cashier. *Did she know what I was doing? Could she see it on my face?* The entire time, he feared that his forced blank expression instead was a stupid grin, a clear signal that he was getting over on Super Valu Saver and that Julep Street's finest rent-a-cops would be waiting for him outside at the Tercel.

At the automatic door, he waited until another shopper was leaving and slipped out on her heels, bracing for an inventory-control alarm that never came. In the parking lot, he wanted to run to the car but dared not do it, compromised as he was by the delicate orientation of the book in his drawers. Once in the car seat, he held fast to the steering wheel and waited for his breath to settle out, and then he went home to Hector. The dog chewed the toy into frazzled cottony bits as Carson told the story, his pulse quickening and his hands gone clammy again.

"It was awesome, boy, just awesome." He swooped down and tousled Hector's head, which the old dog acknowledged with a quick glance up followed by renewed feasting on the toy. "I mean, I didn't even think of doing it until I was right there. A eight-ninety-five paperback. I mean, it's stupid and all, Hector, but I just thought, you know, they take so much, why shouldn't I take from them? So I grabbed it and stuffed it down my pants. That's what I did. Yeah!"

While Hector ate dinner, Carson climbed under the sheet, closed his eyes, arched his toes and jacked off, at last reaching release as his mind played a kaleidoscope of the fantasies he'd warehoused in thirty-some years of self-service. The tipping point was Lurleen—soft-necked, razor-tongued, bodaciously bosomed Lurleen.

When he awoke with night settled outside his window, he decided he should see her again.

The eggs, runny and warm the way Carson likes them, chop nicely and marry up with the hash browns. Carson lifts heaping forkfuls onto triangular wedges of toast, catching the runoff in the swale between his thumb and forefinger and lapping it up. He folds the toast over as he would biscuit dough for pigs in blankets, and he lifts it to his mouth, consuming it in two *snap-snap* bites. He chases the food with a swig of what used to be coffee—before the three creams and four sugars—and repeats the maneuver with the three remaining toast wedges. After that, he swirls the fork along the plate, gathering the last couple of bites of yolky hash browns, and he eats those, too.

"I like a hungry man." Lurleen is beside the table. Oh, how she glides. "Need anything else, sweetie?"

Carson picks up the corner of the napkin tucked in his collar and dabs where his lips meet. "Hell, darlin', just the combination to your heart." He feels good, corny, and he wonders if he can find some whiskey back at the apartment and feel even better.

Lurleen leans over the table to pull in the soiled dishes, and Carson gets a furtive eyeful of her freckled cleavage. Lurleen catches the leer as she stands, and she says, "I'll be right back." He doesn't even bother to hide his craven longings from the John-Deere-hat-wearing mossback at the table across the way, who offers approval in a missing-tooth grin.

Lurleen walks back toward him, and Carson just rolls it out there, his eyes moving from her face to her bosom to her hips and back again.

She brushes his hand with hers as she sets the printed-out bill on the table.

"I'm off in an hour," she says. "What do you think about that, sugar?"

Carson says what he suspects any man would say—any man pumped full of red blood and sexual frustration, any man who wants much but asks for little, any man who can't remember a woman's touch. He says, "Well, looks like I'm having more coffee after all," and Lurleen curls her lips into a smile and pours him another cup.

Thursday, Early

The taillights of Lurleen's pickup guide Carson's Tercel from upper Julep Street and the Shoney's parking lot through the main shopping district and into downtown, which sits dark and abandoned as it watches over the Ohio. She offered Carson neither an address nor a phone number, just a "follow me," and his anxiety percolates as Lurleen gives scant regard to posted speed limits or generally accepted traffic regulations. She whips through four-way stops and turns against red and races the wrong direction down one-way side streets, and all the while Carson sticks close to her back bumper and occasionally crosses himself, a non-Catholic hedging his bets.

It comes as a mild surprise when she bears left off Donerail Avenue and guns toward the Maxine Brockbirch Bridge.

"Indiana," he says, having expected, given the general direction of their travel, that once Lurleen tired of fracturing motor laws she would head east toward Hancock County. Instead, it's north across the old truss bridge, an engineering marvel of Roosevelt's New Deal. From this height and at this hour, with moonlit views of the shimmering river and the lights that dance on the water's edge, Carson no longer sees the blemishes and pockmarks of the place he has always known as home. Tonight, the city is a subtle jewel, and his love for it wells.

Carson cranks the window halfway down, and the night air spills into the car, raising a prickle on his skin. The smell of the Ohio drifts in, something you get used to if you're a river kid. It's not bad—pleasing, really, the aqua scent and the mud and the river birch, all mingling into an odor that is at once intimate and yet elusive of any definition he can place upon it. Carson appreciates this, too. When July and August come, swinging heat and humidity like a mace, the stench will sometimes be unbearable, an inevitability when every river town from Pittsburgh to points west uses the Ohio as a toilet.

Nearly to the end of the bridge now, Lurleen has opened some distance on him. Carson steps the pedal to the floorboard, an urgency he doesn't often seek from the Tercel. It responds gamely. Just inside the clutches of Indiana, he catches her. Lurleen's left blinker engages, a one-time show of road courtesy, and she veers off the state highway onto a gravel lane hugged tight on both sides by scarlet oaks, their upper reaches lacing together like fingers into a canopy. It's darker now, and for the first time, the weight of uncertainty sits heavy in Carson's gut.

Ahead, the trees pull back from a clearing, and Carson's eyes are drawn to the procession of solar lights that illuminate the small yard fronting Lurleen's single-wide trailer. It's well-tended and welcoming, and Carson gazes at the lilac bushes in front and the hanging pots holding who-knows-what that adorn the small wooden deck. Lurleen is out of her pickup, and she catches Carson staring.

"Come in," she beckons with a howdy-do wave, just another friendly soul offering hospitality and, perhaps, a handjob.

Carson pushes himself out of the Tercel, a steadily more

challenging task as the years and his girth have advanced. *That's what we're here for, right, sex?* Somehow, in the fifteen or so minutes from Shoney's to Lurleen's driveway, Carson has halfway managed to talk himself out of the certainty of her come-on. It seems hopelessly farfetched now, that a cheesy pickup line could lead him here, and he wonders—not entirely in the sway of paranoia—whether she has brought him to a well-appointed abattoir. He imagines the rended flesh of Lurleen's many victims as the richest mulch for her gardens.

As he nears Lurleen, she reaches for his rigid hand.

"Do you want to get high?" she asks.

Lurleen sits at an obtuse angle, her bare legs folded under her on the couch as she leans ever deeper into Carson's space. He drags on the joint and tries to keep his eyes well above the breasts she's tucked into a terrycloth robe. It's a losing fight, and he knows it. She knows it, too.

"What do you do, Carson?" Her voice carries a forced sultry quality that he finds lacking compared with her stiletto-heel-to-the-ribcage directness at the restaurant.

He hands the joint to her. "Nothing."

"Really, nothing?" She inhales deep, then lets the smoke curl from her lips back into the open air and into her nose.

"I was the editor of the *Argus-Dispatch*."

"What's that?"

"The newspaper." *Can she really not know?* His thoughts, already jumbled, have been compromised by the pot, something he's partaken of in his life just enough to be clumsy with it. His time inside Lurleen's trailer has been spent trying to find an orientation point. The marijuana, Lurleen's effective ground game of advancing across the couch until she's nearly in Carson's lap, and the kitsch (*who knew there were so many frog figurines in the world?*) have conspired to undermine his best efforts.

"Didn't something happen with that?" She passes the joint to him.

"Yeah, that's what I'm saying. They shut it down yesterday." He takes a drag. Carson's no recognized judge of such things, but it's pretty damned good pot. Lurleen says she got it from a high school kid up in Rockport. She says she offered the kid cash and a blowjob—this second part is presented with nonchalance, the same way she might tell him what she'd had for lunch—and when Carson's dropjaw gives away his shock at the revelation, she says, indignant, "He's eighteen. I'm no kiddie whore." This has the unexpected effect of solidifying Carson's resolve. He wants her bad.

"Why'd they shut it down?" she asks.

Carson hands the joint back to her to finish it up. "Well, apparently nobody reads it anymore—"

"I sure don't."

"—and nobody advertises in it anymore, and a bunch of people making twelve bucks an hour—"

"Twelve bucks an hour? Damn. How do I get hooked up with a job like that?"

"—are too much of a drain, you know, exercising the First Amendment and shit, so this rich asshole decides instead to build a museum to his daddy. And the son of a bitch wants me to come be the director of the damn thing, a tour guide to my own past. Can you believe that shit?" Carson is high, but he recognizes truth as it tumbles from his own tongue. He wants no part of this, but Benny Haller has nearly sixty thousand reasons to bet he'll take it just the same.

"Wow," Lurleen says, "twelve bucks an hour."

"I was making twenty-six." Carson expects to feel better in financial dominion over Lurleen, but he doesn't.

"Wow. Twenty-six bucks an hour."

"Yeah," Carson says. He advances on her now, turning the

tables. "It was the big time. So, listen, Lurleen, I was wondering, are we gonna fuck or what?"

Lurleen is good at what she does. Carson lies back on the couch, and she kneels on the floor and goes to work on him, sure hands and a forthright mouth bringing him close to climax one, two, three times, but never pushing him beyond the threshold. Each time, she pulls back, and the exhilaration fades. She stands and opens her robe, and Carson watches her, the saddlebag, dotted breasts, the soft belly pinched into misshapen sacs of cellulite, the extra pounds making her most assuredly an innie. And then he looks down to her pussy, shaved bare, the lips turning up from her crotch. She straddles him, grasping his hands in hers and pinning them back to the couch. She drops her face down to his, and she kisses him as she begins to grind. Carson tastes himself on her tongue and smells bacon grease in her hair. She arches her back, and he catches a hard red nipple in his mouth as she grinds harder and faster. It doesn't take long. The tops of his toes turn parallel to the ceiling and his hips lock, and he goes.

She slides off him, their transaction finished. "That's a good boy. I'll be right back."

Carson, quickly gone flaccid, turns onto his belly to hide the shrinking. On the floor next to Lurleen's frog display sits a plush toad, with googly eyes and a floppy tongue, and it stares at him in silent accusation.

Thursday, Dawn

Carson checks his left eye in the rearview mirror. The bleeding along his eyebrow seems to have been stanched. The crude tools he used to arrest the flow—the napkins and the tissue and the old Gin Blossoms T-shirt—lie strewn about the passenger seat, blood-stained. He touches a finger to the swelling flesh. The pain is immense, electric.

That crazy bitch.

He's been sitting in the Super Valu Saver parking lot for a half-hour, replaying the scene. Lurleen, back on the couch, sitting alongside him while he stares down the toad. Her fingers finding his nether regions. His gentle protests. "Come on, Lurleen." The moment when he realizes he's been penetrated with the vibrator and he scrambles away, knocking Lurleen ass-first to the floor. Her loud-enough-to-cut-glass invectives as she advances on him. His pulling-up-pants retreat, backing out the door and tumbling down the deck stairs, face-planting, his eye clipping the sharp edge of a pathway stone, her laughter when she sees him crumpled, and the blood.

"That crazy bitch."

He counts cars in the parking lot. Fourteen. If he's looking for the least auspicious time for a black-and-bloody-eyed man to move through the store, this is it. He leaves the Tercel, and as he does, he catches a full-faced look in the side mirror, and for the first time he sees in the gray wispy hair and the corpulence and the bagged-out eyes the face of his own father. This is what Raymond McCullough looked like that March day in 1978, as he and his only son stood back to back in the kitchen, Raymond slicing pork for sandwiches and Carson preparing the bread and then Raymond slumping to the floor, dead of a heart attack before his head struck the countertop. He looked just like this, save for the butchered eye. Raymond McCullough would have never gotten involved with the likes of Lurleen.

Carson passes through the automatic door and veers right, in front of the unlit checkstands. Behind him, the security guard's walkie-talkie crackles, and Carson hears the guard answer but can't make out what's said. As he slips along the frozen-food lockers, Carson tips his head toward the ceiling and finds the white half-dome, where the security camera is tracking him—or, perhaps, some other part of the store. The opacity of the glass cover keeps that a mystery. He remembers a long-ago story in the *Argus-Dispatch* about how retailers try to stem shoplifting, a word that nobody in the piece used, preferring the euphemistic "shrinkage." Rumor was that Super Valu Saver, with a network of cameras controlled by computer algorithm, could monitor every corner of the store 24/7. *Super Valu Saver officials declined to be interviewed for this article.*

Carson dips his head again and picks up speed, moving deeper into the aisles.

———

In the health care section, he turns his back toward the rest of the store and loosens his belt a couple of notches. He tucks a tube of Neosporin into the front of the khakis and shakes his hips, nestling it down into the crotch. A small box of bandage strips follows.

Carson emerges from the aisle along the back wall. He looks right and sees the security guard from the front door coming up the lane, about fifty feet away. Carson turns left and walks away from him. He fights with himself to keep from looking back. As he ducks into home electronics, he grabs his crotch and adjusts the contents of his pants. He throws a quick look over his shoulder and sees nothing, but he hears the steps coming, the guard's pace out of rhythm with his own as together they bang out a syncopated beat on the floor.

Carson leaves home electronics and makes the loop toward home and garden. He's moving north now. The guard continues to track him. Carson's chest tightens, and he feels a familiar faintness, the same panic attack that would strike sometimes when the *Argus-Dispatch* was in danger of missing its nightly deadline. It's stress, he tells himself. (*Stress? What a surprise!*). His breath flutters. *It's stress, it's stress, it's stress. You're not going to keel over in a Super Valu Saver with ointment in your unmentionables.*

He moves faster now, skipping through aisles diagonally, two at a time, toward the back corner of the store, lawn and garden. The beat of the steps behind him fades as he reaches the lawnmower aisle, the gleaming instruments of yard dominion set out in a row, priced to move in a way that Jeff's Handy Hardware could never match, before Jeff Lawson closed up shop three years ago and promptly killed his wife and his dog and himself.

Carson stops and leans against a support post as he tries to tamp down his heavy breathing.

"Can I help you find anything, sir?"

Carson turns, oh so carefully with the merchandise in his drawers, and looks at his pursuer.

"Just looking."

The guard points. "Got some nice solar lights on sale. Buck-ninety-nine. It's getting to be that time."

Carson follows the man's finger. "Yeah. No lawn. Apartment."

"Then why are you in the lawn care aisle, sir?"

Shit. Shitshitshitshitshit.

"I thought this was tools. Did you move things around?"

"No, sir. Tools are around the corner." He points again.

"My bad."

"Are you OK, sir?" Carson looks at the guard, who touches his own brow and slides his finger across it.

"Oh, yeah, that. Tripped. Stupid."

"It looks pretty bad, sir. You'll want to disinfect it. Might need stitches."

"Yeah, I've got that stuff at home. I mean, not the stitches ... I mean, no, it doesn't need stitches. I stopped the blood. I just, you know, I needed a socket set and—"

"Socket sets are around the corner with the rest of the tools, sir."

"Right. You said that. So, I'll just be going over there now, I guess."

As Carson passes the guard, who tilts slightly left to let him pass, he looks up and squeezes out a smile. The guard, whom he figures for not more than twenty-four or twenty-five, has fire tattoos on both arms that begin at the wrist and burn all the way to his elbows. He doesn't smile back.

Carson approaches the one lit-up checkstand. He carries a Great Neck 54-piece socket and ratchet set, the cheapest one he could find at $13.97. That, offset by the $6.68 he'll save on the pilfered Neosporin and the $3.22 on the bandage strips, means that this adventure in shrinkage will cost him only $4.07. More with sales tax.

The security guard, back at his post, watches from the cart corral as Carson hands the socket set to the pimply faced clerk.

"Find everything all right, sir?"

Carson glances past her to the guard. "Yes, fine."

"Oooh, your eye."

"Tripped and fell. No big deal. What's the damage on this thing?"

She passes the socket set over the scanner. "That'll be $14.81."

Carson reaches for his wallet. His fingers brush the outside of his pocket, and then something occurs to him. He has no cash. He'll have to put it on a card, and a card means a name, and a name means he can be traced, and that potentially means bad things. He pulls back his hand.

"I'm so stupid," he says.

"Why?"

"I left my wallet at home. Can you believe that?"

"It happens, sir. Do you want me to hold the socket set while you go home and get it?"

Carson doesn't just smile. He laughs. He laughs hard and loud and long. The clerk laughs, too, but it's a nervous, placating, please-don't-turn-my-skin-into-a-jacket sort of laugh.

"Yes, please—" Carson looks at her nametag. "—Kendra, hold on to the socket set. I'll be right back."

Kendra slips the socket set onto a shelf under her register. Carson, still laughing, heads for the automatic door. The security guard moves toward him at an angle.

Before the door sits the scanner. Carson squeezes his butt cheeks and thighs together, as if it's common knowledge that scrunched flesh can block a scanner's laser. He begins shuffling through.

The alarm goes off. And though Carson has braced himself for it, he freezes in the moment.

"Sir, please step back behind the scanner." The security guard is just feet away.

Carson wants to reach into his pants. More than anything, he wants to reach into his pants, remove the items from his underwear, make his apologies and a grand bargain. *How about I just pay for these items and buy TWO socket sets and those lovely solar lights you were promoting? Of course I have my wallet. That was a lie. I'm a bad person.* He wants to, but he remembers that the guard has a gun, and in a fortuitous moment of clarity he decides that reaching into his pants would be a Very Bad Thing To Do.

Carson runs. He runs through the open double door, onto the sidewalk that fronts the building. He runs headlong into a shopper on his way into the store, and the man in the Kentucky Wildcats T-shirt and madras shorts and flip-flops splays across the ground, arms and legs wiggling as if he's a turtle on its shell. He runs away from the Tercel, another fortuitous moment of clarity, and away from the guard's urging voice. "Sir, come back. Come back here!"

At the east corner of the store, Carson dares to look back. The security guard is watching him but not giving chase, surely obeying a corporate mandate aimed at reducing liability. He has the walkie-talkie to his mouth. Carson doesn't waste time. He lights out of the shopping center, into the thatched immensity of residential streets and houses behind it.

Thursday, Late Morning

Carson awakes to a face full of Hector's butt. Oh, the dog was petulant when Carson finally got home, breathless and sweaty from a jagged two-mile jog-walk through the neighborhoods and schools standing between Super Valu Saver and the apartment. Carson fed him, praised him, apologized to him, cleaned up the pee stain and the excrement—the two things that Hector, in his nurtured dignity, couldn't countenance. "No more adventures without you, boy," he said, and he meant it, and Hector, a magnanimous dog, was at last inclined to forgive. They went to sleep in a clutch, Hector's head buried in Carson's right shoulder, Carson's free arm wrapped across Hector's torso.

That was four hours ago. Now, Carson pushes himself off the bed and Hector's hindquarters, and a tuft of yellow-gray dog hair comes with him, caught under the flapping edge of his contraband bandage. Carson plucks it away. Hector shifts, rolling onto his back and then to his other side. He moans. Carson walk-wobbles into the bathroom.

The eye is worse than Carson feared. While his shoddy application of the stolen Neosporin and strip bandage has done him no favors, the injury clearly holds its own agenda. The purple-blue flesh around the cut has bloated. Carson braces himself to remove the bandage affixed horizontally across his brow. He counts, aloud, *one, two, three*. He doesn't pull.

"Don't be chickenshit. Just do it." Carson hears the thump from the living room as Hector, a self-centered dog, slides off the bed under the erroneous notion that he's being addressed with such dismissive vulgarity. He whines his way into the bathroom with Carson to lodge his complaint.

One, two, three. Carson pulls. He slams shut his eyes, waiting for the pain that doesn't come.

He opens them again. He catches Hector's stare.

"Let me wash up and dress this and then we'll go, OK?"

Hector shifts his massive body, a battleship with a better turn radius, and goes back to bed.

Thursday, Afternoon

Carson stands on the white marble and looks at his elongated reflection in the gleam, his angry eye distorted and indistinct. Hector sits at his feet. Most people who come to a car lot head straight for the neatly arranged line of automobiles, an act that brings the salesmen stampeding out of their coffee klatches, arms extended and bearing business cards. Carson and Hector, on the other hand, arrived in a taxi and walked, unimpeded, through the front door.

From across the hood of a distant Ford Mustang convertible (color: Gotta Have It Green) a young salesman—Carson figures him for twenty-five at the outside and probably younger—sees them and heads over, his penny loafers clattering on the floor. The young man reaches for his collar and grips the Windsor knot in his right thumb and forefinger, straightening it. Next his hands find his belly for a shirt-tail check and the front of his gray slacks, which he flattens from crotch to thigh.

"Sir, that dog can't be in here."

Hector swishes his tail across the marble.

"Why not?"

"He just can't."

Hector backs up and lifts a leg over a car tire.

"Oh, would you look...Sir!"

Carson turns to the dog and snaps his fingers. "You know better than that." Hector lowers his leg and hangs his head.

"He needs to go out, sir," the salesman says.

"But he's a guide dog."

The tension in the young salesman's constipated face eases just for a blink, then resets. "You're...blind, I guess." He looks at Hector, unleashed, who regards him serenely, and then at Carson, whose eyes are locked on his.

"What I mean," Carson says, "is he'll guide me to another car dealer if you don't chill out." Carson bends his knees and squints at the salesman's nametag. "Bradley." He let's it hang there, and then he cuts off the salesman's protest.

"Listen. I want to buy a car. My dog wants to buy a car. If you won't deal with us, I'll find someone who will."

Bradley's lip quivers, threatening a snarl. He beats it back and re-attaches his well-rehearsed smile. "Of course."

Carson walks toward the Mustang. Hector is on his feet, trailing. Bradley, caught off-guard by the sudden migration, rattles behind them, walking at double speed to catch up.

"I called your service department and asked them to tow in my Tercel," Carson says. "I'd like to trade it in." He sets his butt into the Mustang's hood and releases his weight. Bradley looks queasy. "On this, I think. What would this set me back?"

"Let's step into my office and talk about it," Bradley says.

"You step first. I'll follow."

Bradley clenches his fists and sets them atop the mockery of paperwork. *None of this has followed The Script.* Every night, he practices The Script. He greets. He asks the question, pleasant as pie. "What sort of car are you folks looking for?" He separates them from the keys to the beater they drove into the place and hands it off to the service department, and the marks are all but caught now. "What do you say we take it out for a spin?" he says, and he'll lay odds that when they get back after eight, maybe ten glorious minutes in this beautiful new car that doesn't yet smell like grimy children, they'll be running to his office to make a deal—any deal at all, so long as they never have to sit in the booger-festooned bucket seats of their old car again.

And so The Script goes. "Well, they're saying in service that your car is pretty well worn out, but I think my boss can make some things happen here. Let me step out for just a second. You folks all right? Need anything to drink?" So he ambles over to the glass office two doors down and jaws a bit with Buddy, mostly about the Wildcats, and then he comes back and says, "He'd really like to see you folks in this car. How about twenty-two-fifty for your trade? That's a little more than you were hoping for, isn't it? Like I said, he really wants to do this deal. Now, if we just make it sixty-six payments instead of sixty"—and here he makes a big flourish, crossing out the sixty in the four-square diagram he's drawn on the offer sheet—"and you folks kick in another, say, $500 on the down"—and here's another theatrical revision—"we can put you right at a payment of $292 a month, well under the $300 you've got budgeted." This is the best part of The Script. He crosses out the $300 and, for good measure, runs a squiggle through it in red. In its place, he writes $292 the way John Hancock hisownself would have done it.

"Have we got a deal?" And who would say no, given how magnanimous Buddy and Bradley have been about the whole thing? Plus, look at that monthly payment. It's perfect. Where do we sign?

Every night, Bradley practices The Script, a one-man,

one-act huckster drama. Every morning, he leaves the house carrying a sandbag in his gut, hoping he can remember the steps, hoping this day brings a sale. Since he came back from Kabul, Bradley's just been looking for a break, something to set things in order. It's coming. He can feel it.

Now he looks at Carson, this mangled-eye mothergrabber whom he hasn't liked from the first moment with his "chill out" and his I'm-smarter-than-you grin. No respect. No honor. Didn't want a test drive. His mutt lifted a leg on the showroom Focus. And now he's messing with the paperwork. *This asshole,* Bradley thinks, *is sullying The Script.*

He looks down at his four squares. He tried to fill them in— trade value of the Tercel, the sales price of the Mustang, the down payment and the monthly payment—only to see Carson reach across the desk, pull the paper from under Bradley's pen, whip out his own a red Sharpie (*where the hell did that come from?*) and draw a big 'X' across the page.

"Sir," Bradley says. "I'm just trying to—"

"Lookit here, Brad." Bradley winces. He hates being called Brad. Carson goes on. "We need only two numbers to make this transaction. You tell me what you want for the Mustang. You tell me what you'll give me for the Tercel. That's it. Two numbers, Brad. Let's have 'em."

"Sir, I'm trying to tell you that." Bradley pulls the X'd-out paper back into play. *The hell with this guy.* "A 1993 Tercel that doesn't run isn't going to bring much, maybe—"

"It runs."

Bradley and Carson look to the door. Antonio from the service department hangs off the frame. "Runs good, too. Low miles, only eighty-five-thousand. Good tires. Body's in good shape."

"Thank you, Antonio," Bradley says, and the service man jacks up his eyebrows, nods, and leaves. *The Script. The goddamned Script.*

"So, anyway, you were saying?" Carson hangs his mouth half-open, mocking.

Bradley punches the new values into the Kelley Blue Book website.

"OK, fine, a 1993 Toyota Tercel in miraculously good condition, that had to be towed in here even though it runs just fine, we can offer you $1,300. I'll have to doublecheck that with the boss man, but that's what the computer says."

"The computer says $1,351."

"What?"

Carson leans across the desk and swivels the computer toward him. "Hey," Bradley protests.

"See, right there?" Carson says, pointing. "$1,351. I looked it up before I came. I'm not stupid, Brad."

"Sir, I didn't mean...I mean, look, I was just rounding it off. I didn't intend—also, there's gonna be a charge for that tow, so we've got to—"

"Now that you've wasted my time, Brad, I'm gonna have to insist on $1,500. Go check that with the boss man. Tell him $1,500 and I'll pay $26,000 cash for the balance."

"He'll never go for that. Are you kidding? That's a $31,000 car." Bradley pulls the computer back and stares at Carson with rehearsed incredulity.

"See, Brad, it's disappointing that I had to make an offer to get you to tell me the price. Wasting my time again. So here's my counter-offer: $1,700 for the trade and $25,500 cash for the balance."

"But you just said— "

"My dog's getting bored, Brad." Carson stands, and Hector rises in unison.

Bradley goes to his feet and gathers the paperwork. "I'll take it to the boss. But I'm telling you, there's no way. He'd go twenty-seven-two on a different model, maybe the sedan—hell, the sedan with the luxury package—but he's not doing this. There's no way. Not on the convertible." Bradley's voice trails off as he leaves the office.

Carson sits down, and Hector again flattens out across the industrial carpet of the office. Carson reaches down and strokes his boy's head with his fingers. Hector murmurs happily.

"What do you want to bet he'll do twenty-seven-two, boy?"

Swish, swish, swish.

"You're damned right."

Thursday, Late Afternoon

Top down. Black cherry trees in bloom on Julep Street, fragrant blossoms riding on the breeze. Carson guides the Mustang (sales price: $27,200) toward the apartment. Hector sits in the passenger seat, jowls in the wind, and guards the premium car wax Carson swiped from the service department.

Barry Bowersox blares from the radio.

"Our first day without the *Argus-Dispatch*. Anybody miss it? Anybody? Call 794-1978 and let us know. I gotta tell you, friends, this switchboard usually lights up like a Christmas tree when I ask for calls. Today? Nothing. Crickets. It seems that our not-so-dearly-departed daily rag was irrelevant and unloved. Who's crying? Are you crying? I'm not.

"We have Senator Richard Smithers in the studio today, and I'm guessing he's not crying, either. So, Senator, you're facing a re-election campaign this summer and fall. What does the absence of the *Argus-Dispatch* mean for you?"

Carson punches his new car square in the dashboard.

"First, Barry, thanks for having me on again. It's always a pleasure. In practical terms, it doesn't mean anything at all. We've known for years that the *Argus-Dispatch* is in the tank for the other side, but for most of that time, we had to acknowledge them because that was the best way to get the word out about what we're doing, even if they made it difficult. But now, with Twitter and Facebook and other tools, we can take our message directly to the people. And, of course, there's good old-fashioned shoe leather. I visited all hundred and twenty counties in this state last year, and I'll visit every one of 'em again before November. People in this state know who I am and that I stand with them. I don't need the *Argus-Dispatch* for that."

Carson, at a red light, agitates in his seat. "Fuck you," he says, his words spilling into the gathered traffic. The driver in the SUV ahead of him drops a middle finger out his window.

"But here's my question, Senator: Where do you think the *Argus-Dispatch* went wrong? Was it technology? Changing habits? Or something the newspaper actually did? I have my theories, but I'd like to hear yours."

The senator swings big at the softball.

"They lost faith with their customers, Barry, the good people who live here and read the paper and know that it wasn't telling them the full story. You see newspaper circulation declining all over the country. What's the one thing that most newspapers have in common?"

"You mean besides being dead or dying?"

"Yes."

"Tell me, Senator."

Smithers is in full twang now, his baby-kissing, burgoo-slurping, back-slapping glory. "They're generally run by and edited by people who align with the left. The *Argus-Dispatch* certainly was. When you actively alienate large groups of people who don't embrace your socialistic, constitutionally corrupt message, they're not going to stick around. And they haven't. And now we've seen what happens when they don't."

"Yeah, one of the biggest Republicans in the friggin' state shut it down to build a monument to his daddy, you moron." Carson snarls the words, low and guttural, and Hector cowers in the seat, head down, paws on his snout, butt in the air. Carson punches the dashboard again, just below the air conditioner vents in the center console, and it splits into a jagged canyon of stressed plastic.

"Shit!" Carson tries to push the separated pieces of the dashboard together. They won't go. His mind races to possible explanations for the insurance company, and to the five-hundred-dollar deductible that, after today's purchase, will actually be a considerable drain on his means. *Yeah, damnedest thing, I came out of the store, and somebody's broken my dashboard. Must have been somebody jacking it, huh? I mean, I was just gonna be in there for a few minutes, left the top down, you know, nice day and ...*

Hector whines. "Oh, be quiet," Carson says. The dog crawls to the floorboard. "Not everything is about you, you fucking crybaby."

Hector slumps deeper into the compartment. Carson feels his breath go out, his heart pierced by his own words. He's never spoken to Hector this way, on the precipice of rage, his words wielded like a blunt instrument. Traffic stops again on Julep Street, and Carson is certain that he must be the embodiment of evil in the eyes of his fellow travelers, the ones who rolled down their windows on a hot day and heard him castigate poor Hector. He keeps his focus on the floor, on Hector, and he wishes he could rewind to thirty seconds ago and try again.

"Hector," he coos. "I'm sorry. Dad loves you. Please come back up." Hector blinks from the floorboard.

"Please, Hector."

The dog wedges himself deeper. The space between the seat, the door, and the dash is now a sea of ancient yellow fur.

The car behind Carson honks. Green light.

Carson steps hard on the gas, and the Mustang throws itself down the road. Carson has to brake to keep from riding up the tailpipe of the SUV. He looks to the right, into the face of a skeletal woman with clamorous red hair who hangs halfway out the window of a Chevy.

"You ought to be ashamed of yourself, talking to him like that," she says. "I ought to call the cops."

Hector peeks out upon hearing the voice. He barks at her.

Hector lags outside the apartment, nosing the ground cover. Carson stands at the bottom of the stairs, waiting. He's stuck between deference to Hector's bruised feelings and annoyance at being played, for Hector is nothing if not a dog who knows leverage when he has it. When Carson parked the Mustang, silently disappointed that no neighbors were around to make a fuss over the car, he'd tried cajoling Hector from his hiding place, and the dog had seemed amicable—except that his attempts to emerge from the compartment had served only to knot him up further in a space too small. Carson came around to the passenger side and wedged his arms around Hector's considerable girth, pulling him from the car in a tumble of loose fur and slobber. Hector, coming to rest atop his master, who was back down on the asphalt, made up with a floppy-tongued kiss.

Carson thinks of it again, and he laughs aloud. "Take your time, boy," he says. All around them, Barry Bowersox's words fly silently through the air. Carson is missing it, and he doesn't care. Not much.

Hector drops his snout into a patch of daisies, scaring up a bee that darts at him in a cartoon dotted line, and Hector fends off the aerial attack with bites at the air, *snapsnapsnap*. An admonition gurgles in Carson's throat, but he chokes it down, his curiosity winning out over the knowledge that a mouthful of bee will be a painful lesson for his crusty pup. When Hector was young, maybe two or three, he caught a garter snake in the park, a blink-and-it's-over battle that ended with Hector biting the snake behind the head, whipping him like a sock, and then prancing about, the dead serpent hanging under his nose like a fu manchu.

Hector's uprising sends the bee off to the other, plentiful pickings among the shrubbery. Hector, a better-part-of-valor sort of dog, points his tired body toward the stairs. One at a time, Carson follows him up.

Carson watches the messages roll in, fewer than the day before but still considerable, all asking the same questions. *How are you doing? What are you going to do now? Oh, my God, this is so terrible, did you know it was coming?* All questions he cannot, will not answer in any direct way, because he's not doing well, he doesn't know what he's going to do now, he didn't see it coming—and it's this last one that haunts him most. He didn't see it coming. He never got out of the way. If he were inclined to do an emotional dump, he could tell the guy from *The New York Times*—who has written back to implore Carson to agree to that interview—a few things about immediate, retroactive regret, about realizing you've stayed too long only when someone else cashes you out, about all the signs you have to ignore when the last vestiges of joy are wrung out of a job and you keep trudging in, every day, because you don't have the guts to imagine doing anything else.

Bowersox fills the empty spaces of the apartment with dire warnings of creeping socialism in the form of millions of people delivered into the loving arms of private insurance. It's all white noise as Carson gives the same one-word reply, again and again, to his correspondents: "Thanks."

And then hers shows up.

> *Hi, Carson ...*
>
> *I'm sorry I'm just now hearing about this. The news about the Argus-Dispatch made the paper here, and I just couldn't believe it. It's hard to think of it being gone—and especially of you not being there. You loved it so much. I always think about that, and I've often wished that I loved a job the way you loved yours.*
>
> *This is such an awful thing to make me be in touch. I have so many fond memories of the A-D, of you, of the people who were there at that time, and it's so hard to believe 14 years have gone by.*
>
> *So you know I went back to school, right? I'm in Cincinnati now, doing obesity research at UC. I'm junior faculty, so I don't get to sit in my office all day writing papers and getting grants and all that. I'm down with the rats—literally. In fact, yesterday, we did gastric bypass on a rat. Isn't that wild? It's not what I thought I'd do with my life, but it's important work, and I like the place just fine. It's no A-D, though. The older I get, the more I realize that was a one-time thing and I was fortunate enough to experience it.*
>
> *When you get a chance, drop me a note and let me know how you are, Carson. I sure wish it could have ended differently than it did.*
>
> *—Cara*

Carson blinks and reads it again. And again.

He swivels in the chair, turning into the full-throated populist roar of Barry Bowersox, and looks at his dog. Hector, chin on the foot of the bed, gives attention with lifted eyes.

"Cara Echols, Hector."

One ear perks up, then two, and Carson wonders if Hector remembers how much she loved him—how she would throw a ball for him along the river shore for hours, one after another, Hector tireless and young and rippled with muscle, until at last her arm would give out and Carson would take over. Carson wonders if somewhere, in the years that have piled up in the dog's bones like deadfall, Hector remembers falling asleep with his head in Cara's lap as the late movie faded out. Does hearing her name now flush those memories out for Hector, or are his ears simply responding the same as if Carson had said "dinner," or "go outside," or "the relative humidity is forty-three percent"?

Hector puts his head down and closes his eyes, Bowersox blasts onward, and Carson turns back to the screen.

Hi, Cara ...

He stops. He lifts his hands from the keyboard and sets them on his knees, and he squeezes.

The words won't come.

That never happens.

Friday, Edge of Dawn

The computer casts a half-glow in the darkened room, and Carson plots his course, each step an amalgamation of web searches and printed-out maps and mileage markers. The answer is so obvious, so goddamned obvious, that he can't believe he didn't see it the moment Benny Haller walked back into his life and killed the only thing he loves as much as he does Hector.

The whole idea of mission statements has always struck Carson as useless corporate wankery, and yet the words he put at the top of his notebook after his frenzied departure from the bed look altogether like one:

I am a man with a particular set of skills—skills that still hold value in the world. I alone will determine my course and my destiny. I will not be directed to something I do not wish to do, by money or flattery or anything else. It rests with me. And whatever I do next, I will do it in better harmony with the rest of my existence. I will live, and live well. This is not negotiable.

He sits back, satisfied with his work and his decision. Hector chases rabbits through the loamy meadows of his slumber.

Plotted on a map, Carson's route seems aimless, like a housefly trapped in a small room. Up to Jasper and French Lick and Bloomington. Over to Columbus, Indiana. Seymour on the way back down. New Albany and back across the river to Louisville. What the stops have in common: They're towns that haven't turned on their newspapers, towns where a veteran hand like Carson just might find a place to ply his trade.

The notion came to him in fitful sleep, the realization that the boundaries of his life and what he can do with it don't spring up at the edge of town. *What do I have here, really? A small apartment, an arthritic dog, two parents in the ground at Mount Pisgah Cemetery and a life's work that is about to be encased in mothballs and Plexiglass.* It's not much, he knows, and it's nothing that he can't rebuild and replicate somewhere else.

A smile unwinds as Carson thinks about the other commonality. His route, unconventional as it may be, pushes north and east, toward Cincinnati. Toward Cara. Toward something unresolved. He's reread her note dozens of times now, and he sees the regret between the lines, and he feels it, too. He remembers standing apart from the crowd at Skinny's the night before she left, watching her grace as she said goodbye to her work friends, the place pulsating with that godawful Smashmouth tune. His own farewell with her had come a week earlier, with the arrival of the grad-school acceptance letter. White knuckles on the picnic table outside the *Argus-Dispatch* building as she explained herself through glassy eyes and he feigned magnanimity. The application was sent before they tumbled into this thing, she said, and she had to go. Wesley Reardon would be retiring soon and the top job would be Carson's, he said, and he had to stay. "We'll keep in touch," she said. "Of course we will," he said.

He slept at his own place that night, and she at hers. It's never too early to invoke the detachment.

And now, fourteen years later (and eleven years since the last form-letter Christmas card from Cara), the hole blasted into his life provides a way back to her. *What's the cliché, about the door that opens when another one closes? Damned if it isn't so.*

In the savannah of his own dreams, Hector has caught a rabbit. Carson wheels back to the bed when the old boy whinges, and he snuggles his nose and mouth under his boy's chin and blows hot breath on his fur.

"Road trip, boy. You and me and whatever may come." A front paw reaches out like a steam shovel and finds Carson's chest.

Friday, Morning

The Mustang idles at a downtown stoplight, and Carson conducts a gentle debate with himself about how to proceed. Were the goal simply to get to Jasper—get to Jasper and make a cold call at the *Daily Caller*—he would push on east and cross the Natcher bridge and make the straight shot forty-some miles north. But Carson knows it's more than that. He's heading away on a route of nostalgia, and whatever traffic efficiencies the Natcher introduced when it opened in 2002 are offset by what it took away. Carson's memories run along the two-lane roads and downslopes of the Ohio River, this side and the other, chasing coppertone leaves on the wind in fall, the threatening storms of spring, the sweaty hug of late summer. A time before the Natcher bridge and its easy access, when a trip to Louisville meant a ride deep into small-town Kentucky and Indiana before hooking up with Interstate 64 and the push back across the river. Today, Carson finds himself missing that time of his life, when fun was a long drive with the Lemonheads in the cassette deck—sometimes Louisville for a ballgame, sometimes Evansville for a movie and dinner at Mattingly's. It doesn't matter. The point was to go, and as Carson thinks of it now, he cannot remember the last time he did anything for fun the way he did back then.

When the light changes, he turns north toward the Maxine Brockbirch Bridge, a less direct route but one that lays out peacefully alongside the brittle edges of his recollection.

With the top down, it's cold as the Mustang crosses the Ohio, and Carson wishes he hadn't left the pullover hanging on the kitchen chair. Even Hector, a snout-to-toenail furball, hunkers in the seat and gnaws on the flap of the bandanna Carson wrapped around his neck in a pique of whimsy.

The Ohio is the color of cappuccino as it saunters westward, bound for its termination into the Mississippi at Cairo. Once across the bridge, Carson will turn against the current and push faithfully toward whatever destiny awaits him. *Destiny*, now there's a word, the kind that gets hashed out and exhausted in Carson's little universe of inverted-pyramid stenography and rough-first-draft-of-history writing. How many times has he seen it, used it, willfully oblivious to its hackneyed nature? *Team of Destiny*. He remembers writing that headline for the front page when Kentucky won the basketball championship in 1996, as if it were *fait accompli* that the Wildcats would win it all, entitled as they were to the glories of their sport.

And now, as Indiana pulls him in, Carson's synapses fire and he's not in a newsroom anymore. His thoughts travel to the old house on Worland Street, to his mother's room, where he sits beside her bed, sunshine dripping through the half-open blinds, holding her crinkled-paper hand, listening as she tells him that "Raymond called me on the phone from heaven." It's a surprisingly lucid sentence from a woman almost fully given over to the dementia shredding her brain. He sees himself inside the memory, sees himself say, "Yes, Mom," and he can't help thinking of the previous summer, escaping to the movie theater on a suffocating day and watching Forrest Gump sit with his own dying momma and receive her treacle about destiny.

Carson looks over at his dog. "Hollywood. What a bunch of bullshit." Hector, an understanding dog, cocks his head wisely, and Carson gives him a noogie and straightens the bandanna.

As Carson passes the turnoff for Lurleen's single-wide of amphibian horrors, he gooses the Mustang, and she responds with a fulsome roar. Hector sits up and filters the air through his teeth as they haul ass toward Rockport, and beyond.

Friday, Noontime

Bill Drummond's choice of restaurant, Shoney's, says there will be no job for Carson. Oh, sure, Drummond had been happy to see Carson drop in cold to the newsroom. It had been handshakes and back claps between a couple of guys who certainly were friendly if not actually friends. That esteem was a byproduct of directing staffs that competed on a handful of southern Indiana stories back before Mantooth Media closed the Rockport bureau. Just another paper cut on the *Argus-Dispatch*'s calliope ride to obsolescence.

Carson follows Drummond on his heels, and Drummond follows the hostess, and Carson knows you don't take a real prospect to Shoney's. You take him somewhere local, somewhere distinctive, like the Schnitzelbank. You show off your town a little bit. When Carson had the jobs to give, that's how he did it. Shoney's or Fazoli's with the ones who weren't going to make the cut. The Woodwind for the ones he'd send home with an offer.

The men drop into the opposite booth seats, bountiful bellies jostling the table to clear space. The standard-issue middle-age server is fast with the glasses of water, and Carson can't help but wonder if there's a kid in Jasper she blows for weed.

"What happened to your eye?" Drummond asks.

"Dog stepped on my head when I was sleeping."

"Really?"

"Sure."

"Damn. Well, OK, so you're looking for a job."

"Yep. Time for a new start. Got one?"

Drummond is too fast with the reply. "Wish I did." His grin comes out sideways, and Carson feels silly for having come and wonders why Drummond didn't just deliver his regrets while walking him back to the Mustang.

"Fact is," Drummond says, "we're shedding through attrition. I come to work every day hoping that nobody quits me, especially a reporter. Between you and me, the desk is gonna be gone soon anyhow. Corporate's putting in these regional editing hubs—three of them—to handle production on all thirty-seven papers."

Carson sips his water and considers the end of Drummond's bulbous red nose and notices its not-insignificant resemblance to the dildo Lurleen used to violate him—a thought that causes him to choke on his drink as he stifles laughter.

"You OK?" Drummond asks. Carson holds up a hand in the affirmative and sputters out the last of his coughs.

He can't account for why Drummond would tell him something he obviously hasn't shared with his own people. It's the curse of the modern newspaper manager to carry such odious and destructive knowledge when corporate finds newer and shittier ways to squeeze the blood out. Bill Drummond, the pitiable bastard, probably needs to purge it to avoid being irretrievably corroded. The lunch invitation makes sense, in that it's as much confessional as interview. Carson gets it. He'd have loved to unburden himself of the fetid water he used to carry for Mantooth.

"So no local editing?"

"Well, me and Dick Beverly, my city editor. But ... yeah."

If there's one thing Carson can be sure of, it's that some production monkey in Manitowoc isn't going to know the first fucking thing about Jasper, Indiana—its history and its peculiarities, the kinds of things that good editors cultivate and revere, and the kinds of things good copy editors know as surely as they know that two and two is four. The inevitability is a sloppier, less reliable publication.

"Jesus," Carson says. "That's really going to hurt, isn't it?"

Drummond screws up his mouth as if he's preparing to deliver the corporate-mandated rebuttal of such a contention, a screed propped up on such phrases as "more with less," and "streamlining" and "efficiencies." Mouth half-open, he merely mumbles. "Yeah."

"It's such a different place now," Drummond says now, and then he's interrupted as the server scoots up to the table for the orders. Drummond takes a bacon cheeseburger and fries, and Carson makes it two.

"Anyway, we're all about the web nowadays, even though it doesn't pay for hardly anything. We talk metrics and pageviews and SEO—a year ago, I didn't know what the hell SEO is, and now I obsess about it—and all kinds of other shit. A two-hundred-word story about some poor cracker who runs his car off 231 is more valuable, in this new world of ours, than anything else we do. Last year, we did this three-part series on the Indiana economy—real nuts-and-bolts stuff about how we've weathered the storm here in Jasper better than they have elsewhere. Hoo boy, I wouldn't want to be running a newspaper in Elkhart, let me tell you. Anyway, graphics, sidebars, the works. I think maybe four people commented on it online, it got shared maybe a dozen times on Facebook. But if some asshole beats on his kid on St. Charles Street, the Internet blows up."

He and Carson look at each other. The shared, unspoken knowledge is that they've had equivalent experiences. The fact is, they could call five other newspaper editors, pull them in from Evansville and Seymour and Elizabethtown and Terre Haute and New Albany, and it would be the same story, again and again. Drummond isn't telling Carson anything he doesn't know. The only difference—and it's a significant one—is that Drummond's newsroom is still alive.

"You sure you want to get back in?" Drummond assaults the ketchup bottle as he speaks, and at last he gets it to flow onto his just-arrived plate. "I heard a rumor the severances were pretty good down there. Might be a chance to walk away, live like a normal person."

Carson presses down on his burger with two fingers and cuts it in half. "I'm forty-eight years old, Bill. I know how to do one thing really well. I'm not ready to pack it in."

"You've got a problem, though." Drummond dunks his napkin in his water and dabs at a spot of ketchup on his tie. "No market for what you do really good. You know what my publisher says about editing? He says, 'If it's wrong, we can fix it later. Get it up there on the site.' And I say, yeah, well, what about the print edition? There's no fixing that later. He just kind of smiles but he doesn't say anything. He's looking down the road, when the presses won't turn anymore and he's not paying $3.62 a gallon in gas to carry the paper around to the driveways and pay boxes. It's still the biggest source of money, but it's dying. He knows it. I know it. Shit, you can't not know it if you're in this thing."

Carson pushes his plate to the middle of the table. Drummond, mouth full, keeps going. "Now, if you knew how to optimize our presence in the social sphere, I might have something for you. That's a direct quote, by the way, 'optimize our presence in the social sphere.' My website guy said it. The only hire I've been able to make in three years, and he talks in riddles. Every day, he brings me this printout that shows what people are doing on our site, the stories they're reading, how long they're lingering on a page. He's been trying to get me to use that to make decisions about what goes on the front page of the actual newspaper, but I'm resisting, because I think the audiences are different and because, dammit, I'm just old-school enough to think that newspapers ain't TV, that you gotta give people what they need to know in addition to what they want. He's a good kid. Earnest. Hardworking. Got a little wife and they just bought a house, so they'll be here awhile, I think. But, damn, I don't understand him half the time. He thinks we should have come out against building a new library. Says they're obsolete." Drummond pulls a fry from the lagoon of ketchup on his plate. "I don't know. I don't understand the world he lives in."

The server sweeps by again. Drummond asks for the check. Carson asks for a box.

Drummond pulls in a deep breath, holds it, then drops it on the table.

"I'm going to walk in one day and find out he's got my job," he says.

Carson reaches across the table and snares a fry off his host's plate. He folds it into his mouth. "At least you've got a job to lose."

Hector tears into his lunch, using his snout to push the box along the walkway as he chases every last succulent smattering of grease and ketchup. Carson spreads the *Daily Caller* out on his lap and begins his assessment. The skybox atop the front page heralds a victory by the Wildcats baseball team against Castle: THE RIGHT STUFF. It's corny and clichéd and right over the top of the head of anybody born after 1985, and Carson's revulsion is moderated by the grudging knowledge that he's used such pop-culture mile markers in a similar way more times than he'd care to acknowledge. To the extent that he has an ethic about such things—and daily journalism, in his experience, is far more about pushing it out the door than adherence to craft integrity—Carson tries to bring a bit of artistry to the borrowing of others' phrases. He remembers a lunar eclipse some years back, and a front-page standalone photograph of a kid standing on his balcony with a telescope oriented to the stars. He wrestled with that one longer than he should have, looking for just the right words, rejecting the ones that came easily—THE STARS AT NIGHT... or WHEN YOU WISH UPON A STAR... He studied the photograph again, looking for something, anything, to shake his brain. Jolly called over, putting him on the clock: "Boss, you done with that? I gotta get this page going." Carson waved him off and bore down again. Finally, inspiration blessed him, and Carson wrote his headline: A MARVELOUS NIGHT FOR A MOON GLANCE. A cut above, and he knew it as he released the photo to the page. Here's Jolly, a moment later: "Damn, that's really good."

The sun perches overhead, and Carson puts the paper down and stretches his arms across the back of the bench and turns his face into the tumbling rays. The coolness from the morning is burning off in the early afternoon, and Carson's arms tingle in the extension. He's antsy to get down the road toward his other targets. The disappointment at finding rejection in Jasper hangs on him, and he wishes momentarily that Drummond had said yes, that he could come back to this spot along the river every day, filling his ears with songbirds' stanzas while watching Hector plod back and forth across the path. Carson wishes that, and in the next moment he's self-aware enough to know that Jasper, alone, could never make him the sort of guy who partakes of something so quaint as river walks. When is the last time he took Hector down to the Ohio, burbling mightily just three blocks from his apartment door? He can't remember it. Hector probably can't, either. Carson figures what's wrong with him requires more than a new town. It's going to have to be a new way of living. *Can I get that at forty-eight? Can anyone at any age?*

Carson picks up the sports section, and a flash of gold finds his eye. Hector, packed to the ribs with cheeseburger, pounces at a squirrel. It's a quick first move, surprising given the dog's infirmities, and Carson watches agape as Hector gives chase. The squirrel zips left and right and back again, as if on the end on a string, and the mobility is too much for Hector, whose legs cross up and send him sprawling onto the brown-grass greenbelt. Carson launches from the bench to Hector's side, and the squirrel alights on the branches of a river birch and chatters at them.

"Are you OK, boy?" Carson says. He kneels beside Hector and brushes back the fur atop his head. The dog is a bit wild-eyed. His tongue hangs sideways from his mouth as he pants. Carson touches his nose to Hector's, feels its wetness, and the the dog grumbles, a blast of warm bacon breath behind it, and he slips his tongue between his master's lips. Carson sputters and pushes himself to his feet.

"I'm not that desperate, boy. Yet. Come on, let's go."

Carson retrieves the emptied box and deposits it in the can beside the bench.

"Come on, boy."

Hector straightens his front paws and uses them like pistons to propel his head, neck and chest off the ground. Back legs wobbling, he brings his ass end up behind. Safely up on four legs, he shambles over to Carson, waggy-tailed.

Carson stoops and straightens the bandanna and uses his hands to brush grass and dirt from Hector's coat. The Mustang waits up ahead, strident green in the sun.

The Balance of Friday

*S*prings *Valley Verifier* owner and editor Gary Grundle slips his thumbs inside his suspenders and snaps them against his rump-roast chest. "I need a clerk, and fast."

"A clerk?" Carson says.

"Yep." *Snap.* "You know, wedding announcements, obits, calendars, stuff like that." *Snap.*

"I was hoping for something...I don't know, meatier. I edited a bigger paper. Could do some good work for you."

Snap. "Yep. Shame about that." *Snap.* "This is what I got."

Indiana, collectively, has always struck Carson as a bit inscrutable, a place that defies the conventions of westward expansion and builds its towns at the intersections of the road grid, their economies hinging on the prospect of selling a soda to a passerby. French Lick, though, is different, a town of wineries and resorts, held in the embrace of lush forestland and off the radar of a faceless, destructive force like Super Valu Saver.

87

A place that could be home, maybe.

Carson asks the question: "How much?"

"Eight-fifty, twenty-four hours a week, no benefits."

"You expect people to live on—" Carson trundles through the math. "—two-hundred and four bucks a week?"

"No, no, of course not." *Snap.* "You'd need another job. Linda was slinging pizza at Pluto's. Met Tyler there." Grundle sneers, saying "TY-ler" the way a girl with a turned-up nose would. "They're off to Chicago, and I'm screwed." *Snap.* "By the way, what happened to your eye?"

"Got hit by a foul ball at a baseball game."

"Tough break." *Snap.*

Bloomington, 3:13 p.m.

Veronica Vickers sends a message to Carson through the reception desk. "In meetings all day. Sorry."

Carson leans on the Formica countertop in the lobby, trying to make all friendly-like with the clerk at the *Bugle*. "Have any openings?"

"Gosh, I don't know." She pushes her glasses up the bridge of her nose. Carson sucks in his overhang.

"What about in the newsroom?"

"Gosh, I don't think so."

"Nothing?"

"I don't think so." She smiles, and Carson notes that one front tooth is slightly longer than the other. *Fix that, change or lose the glasses, do something about the broken-out face, and you've got a woman instead of a girl*, he thinks. "The journalism grads at IU snap them up pretty quick. Say, what happened to your eye?"

Carson finds the ring on her left finger. "Kissed a woman who wasn't my wife. Got beat up."

"You deserved it, then."

"I'm just kidding. I walked into a door. Listen, do you like Vickers?" He doesn't know the new editor. When the job came open in Bloomington last October, he applied for it—as did every other unhappy newspaper editor in the Midwest, he figures. Carson didn't even get a courtesy call, and when the job went to a twenty-eight-year-old Syracuse grad, the uncharitable assessments spilled from editor-to-editor emails and across the comments section of the *Bugle* website.

"Why?" The clerk, no longer smiling, rolls her chair back a foot or so.

"Just wondering. Come on, between you and me."

The clerk looks right and left and then back to Carson. "She's a witch."

"A witch?"

"A bitch."

"Really?"

"Yes, really."

"Why?"

She rolls forward. "Listen, mister, do you have some business here? Do you want a subscription or something?"

"No, I'm just passing through."

She adjusts her glasses. "Well, can we be done? I'm going to get fired if I keep talking to you."

Columbus, 4:36 p.m.

Delbert McGuinn pushes half a sub sandwich across the desk, a charitable act.

"No, thanks," Carson says. "I had a hamburger with Bill Drummond a few hours ago."

"Drummond!" Bits of gnashed-up cheese spray from the corners of McGuinn's mouth. "Could you hear his arteries clogging? That fat fuck."

Carson smoothes his shirt over his own protuberance. McGuinn starts in again.

"So you're making the rounds, are you? Jasper, French Lick. Where else you been today?"

"Bloomington."

"Bloomington!" A scrap of lettuce escapes McGuinn's mouth and falls to the desk. He sweeps it away with his free hand. "Any of 'em have jobs?"

"Would I be here if they did?" Carson inches the sandwich back across the desk.

"Good point. Well, I got a job. Yes, sir. Hey, what happened to your eye?"

"Somebody threw a cat at me. A job?"

"You're a funny guy. Yep. Sports editor. My guy's leaving for Dayton in two weeks. Gonna cover the college there. Doesn't that beat all? He can run his own shooting match here, but he's going to Dayton. Good kid. I'm gonna miss him. Need somebody quick, and good."

"Dayton's a good place."

"It's a fucking shithole."

"Yeah."

McGuinn pokes the last bite into his hole like he's packing a gunbarrel. He looks Carson over. Carson sits up straighter.

"You know anybody?" McGuinn asks.

"Yeah. Me."

"You want to cover sports?"

"Absolutely."

"You covered sports before?"

Carson watches the corners of McGuinn's eyes, crinkled in mirth. *The bastard is having fun with me.* "Absolutely. I came up through the sports department." This is what Raymond McCullough would have called "a lie whiter than Bill Monroe." Carson spent one semester as sports editor at the college paper, and that's only because clear precedent held that every editor of the Murray State *News* passed through sports on his or her way up the chain, and when Carson McCullough was twenty years old, he wanted nothing more than to be editor of the school paper. Such single-minded pursuits had been, in more recent years, the cause of considerable retroactive consternation. In the cold glare of hindsight, he often wished he'd channeled that ambition toward getting inside Lisa Dunham's pants. At a school reunion a few years back, Lisa—now Lisa Grant, and not so blonde or so thin or so porcelain in her beauty—had revealed the same wish by whispering lonely housewife fantasies into Carson's ear while her husband was in the can.

"How old are you?" McGuinn says.

Carson touches his sideburns—left, then right—as if he could dab out the gray. "Delbert, I don't know how to tell you this—"

"Yeah, yeah, illegal and shit. Humor me. I'm just spitballing here."

"I'm the youngest forty-eight-year-old you know."

McGuinn lifts the wrapped-up half sandwich and drops it into the metal wastebasket beside his desk. Carson looks at the editor but doesn't see him. He's focused instead on the countertop behind McGuinn, strewn with newsprint whose efficacy had faded by the time it came off the press. On the back wall, over McGuinn's right shoulder, hangs a whiteboard subdivided into ten squares, each one dated, only three of them filled with plans for coverage. Pedestrian coverage, at that. City and county meetings and spoonfed crap from the hospital that a half-decade ago, in his own newsroom, Carson would have turned away without a thought. As bodies disappeared from the newsroom even with the daily paper and the website demanding constant feeding, he learned to stop looking askance at a weaksauce feature. Each one, no matter how slight or outright bad, moved matters a little closer to the end of the day.

At once, the notion that Carson has been dodging on Indiana byways runs smack into him. He doesn't want just any newspaper job, and certainly not the one being dangled here for Delbert McGuinn's amusement. He wants his job, the job he's more qualified to do than any person on the planet, the one that was shot out from under him by Benny Haller. He wants it despite all the corners he's trimmed off and all the biddies who send in tremor-handed letters assailing him for the split infinitives and all the top-down corporate dictates and everything else. He's sick to his stomach as he realizes that he prefers being comfortable and afflicted at his old job to the uncertainty of someone like Delbert McGuinn. And he's sicker still to know he can't have it.

"The last two kids I've had in here were twenty-five and twenty-three," McGuinn says. "Go-getters. Those boys would come in early, work the phones, write me a blog item or two—we're real big on the blogging here—and go out and cover a game, come back here and do their pages. Lather, rinse, repeat, baby. I told 'em that if they worked hard here, good things would happen, and damned if I wasn't as good as my word. Perry's up at the Milwaukee paper now. Jim-Ray's headed for Dayton, like I said. Good boys. Didn't sleep. Ate and breathed this place. You think you're ready for that?"

Carson doesn't process the question, which matters not because he figures McGuinn doesn't expect an answer. Carson's thoughts are on Hector, asleep in the back seat of the Mustang, and on Seymour and New Albany, places he now won't be stopping, and on the motel room waiting in Louisville, and on Cara, in Cincinnati, just a day away.

Carson stands and smoothes his shirt again, and he offers a handshake.

"Thanks for your time, Delbert."

"You bet. Good talking to you."

Carson is almost through the door and into the low din of the newsroom when the question comes. "Hey, let me ask you something. Rumor is that Haller dropped a year's pay on you. That true?"

"Yeah."

"Well, if you don't mind me asking, what the fuck are you doing here? Drag your ass to a beach and stay there."

Carson smiles and lifts a fingertip, whisking the corner of his mouth. "You missed a spot, Delbert."

Louisville, 6:37 p.m.

Hector, offended by the offer of motor lodge tap water, sulks until he hears the snap-and-pullback of the salmon and rice. He catches dinner in airborne nibbles as Carson empties the can into his dish.

"You worked up a powerful hunger, riding in the car, doing nothing." Hector, a prideful dog, stops his feast long enough to give Carson the kind of stare practiced by old married couples, and then he starts in again with the wolfing.

Carson tugs on his shirt from the back of the neck, pulling it over his head, and as it slips his skin he catches a sideways glance in the mirror. The body is not one he recognizes. He has become an old person, and quite before his time, his arms thin and without terrain, the muscles sunken below sallow skin. His belly tumbles like a rockslide over his belt buckle, and his ass— well, there's no ass to speak of. His backside has gone concave, pushing north. He flashes on a memory of the *Argus-Dispatch* as he loved it so many years ago, and of Cara. Reardon comes out of his office, fifty years old, a fossil by Carson's reckoning, squinting into the newsroom with befuddlement, as Reardon so often did. Carson had never been alone in noticing that the old editor, when he stood erect, looked like a parenthesis. Carson rolls his chair to Cara, sitting next to him on the copy desk, and intones in Reardon's baritone, "Has anyone seen my ass?" Cara snorts and buries her head under her arms on the desk. Carson, biting the inside of his lip to keep from letting go his own peal of laughter, says, "Need anything, boss?" Reardon, eternally oblivious, grins through the confusion. "No, no. I—" And back into the office he goes.

Carson now regards the image in the mirror. "You're Wesley Frickin' Reardon, you miserable slab of skin."

Hector throws a high-pitched yawp.

"Not you, silly."

Carson pulls a sweaty longneck from the box and tumbles back onto the bed, wiggling his hips to move himself to the far side and out of the accusing reflection. He leans back across to the nightstand and retrieves his keychain and the attached churchkey. A clean jerk, and the Budweiser is there for the taking. Carson sets it down beside the bed and goes back for the phone.

Hector sidles up by the nightstand and swishes his tail.

"Give me a minute, boy."

Hector gripes as he settles into the carpet.

On the third ring, there's a pickup and a greeting—"*Times*, Dempsey"—and Carson swallows the bile that has moved in under his clavicle.

"Dan, it's Carson McCullough."

At once, the terse voice turns jocular. "Hey. Hey! Damn, man, good to hear from you. What are you up to?"

Carson picks up the beer and sets it against his belly. "You remember where we took Annette and that friend of hers—shit, what was it, Darlene? No, that's not it—"

"Raylene."

"Raylene. Yes. Anyway, after getting cut loose, I figured I'd do some traveling. So I got in the car and drove on out."

"You're here in Louisville? At the fucking Paddock Motel?"

"Yep."

"I didn't even know that place was still around. It was a dump in '85."

"I think I got the same room. Not sure anybody's been here since us. I found your condom wrapper on the floor."

"Keep it. It'll probably fit your tiny pecker."

"The head, maybe."

Dempsey busts out a belly laugh, and it's instant comfort, the resumption of a conversation that started at freshman orientation and has continued, in fits and starts and long-distance phone calls and honest-to-goodness letters when such things existed and later email and the occasional face-to-face and handshake at some press association luncheon or Murray State reunion. It's the gift of the familiar, and something Carson knows he has been denying himself.

"It's funny that you called," Dempsey says. "I'm editing our Sunday centerpiece. It's about the *Argus-Dispatch* and what it means for the rest of us—the rest of us being those who haven't been smart enough to get out before the ax comes for us. You're in here, too."

"I am?"

"Yep. 'Repeated calls to Carson McCullough, the *Argus-Dispatch* editor at the time of its closing, went unanswered.' You want to help me fill in the blanks?"

"Uh, no." Distance sets in. The question from Dempsey comes fast and bloodless, just the way Carson would want a reporter to approach a source—and precisely the opposite of what he wants to hear from his old buddy now.

"Not for attribution?" Dempsey asks, a hopeful lilt in his voice.

"Off the record entirely."

"Yeah, shit, OK. Karen'll just have to put my dinner in the fridge."

C arson detaches the bottle from his naked midsection, his tummy going elastic and then snapping back into place. An hour goes by fast when you're telling how your life ended.

"You're crazy," Dempsey says. "A year's pay in hand and your full salary to be a docent? And you haven't said yes?"

"It's not a docent, Dan. It's executive director. What do I know about that?"

"Nothing. But you know everything about the newspaper business. You're the perfect guy for this. You shouldn't be tooling around at rinky-dink little papers. Jasper? Columbus? Come on. You were better than that twenty-five years ago."

"I know."

"I mean, that's bush league stuff."

"I know. Look, man, I know it sounds stupid to complain, but this has really messed me up. Yeah, the job had gotten shitty, and was getting progressively shittier, but I liked the work. I miss it. I don't know what I'm going to do without it. You think that sounds all stupid and saccharine, whatever. That's the way it is, all right?"

"OK."

"What're you gonna do when it's over at the *Times*?"

"If."

"Yeah, well, I don't believe in if anymore."

Dempsey is quiet, and Carson knows he has a nerve in his grasp. They came out of school together, Carson the final-semester editor of the Murray State *News*, Dempsey his second in command. Change one little detail, and maybe it's Dempsey in a rattletrap motel, a warm beer at his side, making this call to Carson, who's trying to put a Sunday special to bed so he can go home and kiss the family. That spring, before graduation, the two of them were up for the same jobs, along with every other journalism grad in the state. *The Times*, the big, family-owned behemoth in Louisville, had a suburban reporter's spot open, a just-so match with Dempsey's skills. Carson, the better copy editor of the two, ended up at the *Argus-Dispatch* and filled an open spot on the desk. And much to the surprise of both, neither ever left, the promotions and inertia coming fast enough to keep them both satisfied, or comfortably numb.

"Karen and I, we've actually talked about this." Dempsey's voice is low, almost imperceptible amid the white noise of a newsroom and a cheap motel's window AC unit. "I mean—shit, man, I know I should be ready for it, but I'm not. This is what I do, and this is where I live. Whatever I do, it'll be here. Kids in school. Jenell wants to go to UK—that's ten grand a year. We're gonna swing that, but just barely. We got a mortgage. Karen, she's got a good job at Kosair. I think—I think we'd be all right. Shit, I don't know. Goddamn, man, you're making me depressed."

"Not my intention."

"It's goddamn eight-thirty."

"Sorry."

"I gotta go."

"I want to talk about this some more."

"Yeah, I've been wanting to talk to you, too. Come by Monday? Say, eleven?"

"Monday will work."

"All right. Have a good rest of your trip, whipdick."

"Give Karen a squeeze for me, scrotum lips."

Saturday, Early Morning

Carson awakes, flailing, to what sounds like an asthmatic man hacking up a lung.

On the floor between the foot of the bed and the television set, Hector stands on quivering legs and stretches his neck like a turtle's and hacks away.

Dinner expels from his mouth in a single globule, sliding off his tongue and onto the floor in a dollop. The odor of processed fish marinated in stomach acid tangos into the small room, and Carson covers his nose and mouth with the collar of his undershirt.

The energy required to back up his digestive process saps Hector, and his legs betray him. Carson kneels beside the dog, impromptu surgical mask still in place, and smoothes the shag atop Hector's head.

"Are you OK, boy?"

Hector looks at his man, glassy-eyed. Carson palms his snout. Dry. He can't remember now if the dog touched his water.

Carson pushes himself up and heads to the bathroom. He

stoops to pick up Hector's dish and dumps the warm water into the sink. The spigot on, he scrubs the inside rim of the bowl with his finger and then rinses it. He turns on the cold-water flow and refills the dish. He slips his right hand over the bowl, gripping the outside edge with all five fingers as if palming a basketball. His left hand finds the towel rack and pulls down a wash rag that has a frayed, embroidered horse galloping across its terrycloth plain.

"Here you go, boy." Hector noses the dish. The water sloshes. "*Drink*, Hector."

The dog belly crawls until his head is above the lip of the bowl. He drops his tongue into the water and takes it in. Tongue-curled water finds Hector's mouth and dots the carpet around the bowl. Carson stoops and uses the wash rag as a glove, picking up the clumpy vomit. His hand full, he steps sideways to the sink and washes out the rag. The congealed, half-digested dog food falls to the ceramic sink and separates into smaller chunks, mudlike in consistency, and eventually cedes to the flow of water pushing it toward the drain.

Hector has finished drinking and now lies on his side. Carson returns and scrubs out the obvious evidence. With an underhanded throw, he puts the rag into the sink.

"Two points, boy." Hector's tail swishes as if swatting a slow-moving fly.

Carson lowers himself to the floor and stretches out behind Hector. He places a hand on the dog's ribs and runs his fingers along the xylophone bones to the breast and back again. Hector's tail moves in rhythm, a conductor's wand directing a waltz.

"A long day for you."

Carson sets his head onto his right shoulder, his mouth behind Hector's upturned left ear.

"A long day for both of us."

Carson exhales, and the ear flaps twice. Hector wipes a paw

across his snout. Carson wriggles forward and up so he doesn't irritate the dog further.

"We're going to see Cara tomorrow. Do you remember Cara?"

The ear perks and then flattens.

"We're going to figure this out."

Hector closes his eyes.

"We always figure it out."

Carson lifts his head and sets his chin on Hector's exposed jowl. The dog shoots out his tongue, lickety-split, and catches Carson in the nose with a kiss that sends him, sputtering, to his former position.

"So you're saying you love me, boy?"

Hector's tail pounds out two beats on the carpet.

"I love you, too."

Carson slips an arm around his dog and holds on. When Hector at last falls into rumbling slumber, Carson doesn't hear it. He has already slipped his own consciousness, into that sweet in-between that buffers awareness and the madhouse mirrors of deep sleep. There, little Hector rambles on the sun-scorched apartment lawn on the day Carson brought him home. He's all outsized feet and flopping ears and limitless energy, a pup who will spend the next month waking Carson at three a.m. to carry him downstairs for a pee and playtime. In pre-dream reverie, Carson sees his boy gather the branch of a blue ash in his mouth, the eight leaves hanging limp from the stalk. Hector gallops happily across the yard until he trips over his quarry, tumbling ass over teakettle and then looking around as if the world he knows has somehow played him for a fool. At last, he finds his way to four feet and noses the traitorous leaves, unsure whether to give them another chance at being conquered.

Dreamland Carson slaps his hands on his knees and little Hector does a leaping one-eighty and now is running, running, running...

Saturday, Late Morning

The simple green sign perched on the shoulder of Interstate 71 comes at Carson like a spring storm, unnoticed until it's on top of him and there is no escape from the torrent.

SITE OF
FATAL BUS CRASH
MAY 14, 1988

Carson swings toward the inside lane, then jerks the Mustang back when he hears the angry blast from an eighteen-wheeler bearing down. Past the sign now, he checks the side mirror and makes his move, sliding across the two lanes and into the green-grass swale separating the northbound and southbound asphalt. His right arm shoots out, a safety bar to hold Hector in place as the car chews turf on the U-turn. The Mustang oriented, Carson guides her onto the southbound lanes, across to the outside shoulder, and noses her forward until she sits perpendicular to the companion sign.

Nearly twenty-four years clear of that horrible night and the interminable days that followed, he's seeing the site for the first time. Some people make pilgrimages to those places where human catastrophe has played out, yielding either to a latent need for connection or a ghastly fetish for suffering. Dobber, bless him, had his picture taken here, an unfathomable tastelessness in Carson's estimation. Carson has always thought it better to practice avoidance, going out of his way at times to avert being where he is right now, facing his own memories.

Here where the Mustang idles, twenty-seven lives met their end on a school bus choked with poisonous smoke and flames, the result of a fuel tank that exploded when a wrong-way driver in a pickup plowed headlong into the bus in the rising night.

They were asleep, most of them, and they were kids, most of them. Ninety-some miles from home, exhausted from a day's wonderment at Kings Island, the members of a church group—twenty-four children and three adults—perished in a human mass that could find no way off the bus, forward or back.

Carson, his hand still on Hector and kneading the loose skin on the old dog's neck, looks out across the median at the monuments, ornate and simple, that have continued to spring up all these years, like seasonal blooms to mark not renewal but death—final and unflinching death.

His mind is untethered now, and he closes his eyes and tries to remember 1988, as if he could just will it to return. He can't, of course—like so many other things, it's too far gone, the fashions and the peculiarities of speech and the fads lost to the swirl of memory. But this one precise thing, this bus crash memorialized with understated plainness, has never been far away.

Carson was twenty-four when it happened, not much older than some of the kids whose promise ended that night. Reardon's phone call the next morning—*at seven fucking a.m.*, Carson complained until the horror became clear—set a surreal, nightmarish, sleep-deprived week in motion.

"Get in here," Reardon had said. "There's been an accident. Holy sweet Jesus, a guy drove the wrong way on I-71 and killed a bunch of kids."

Time has a way of buffing the edges of high-definition memories. Forty-eight-year-old Carson can't remember what twenty-four-year-old Carson said to that order, or to much of anything else that day. Soon enough, the horrible math made itself clear to everyone at the *Argus-Dispatch*, and they all did what the job dictated. They swallowed their own sense of horror and their latent fears, for themselves and for their families, and they set about the work.

Reardon, whose preternatural lack of aggressiveness had set off innumerable beers-after-work rants by Carson, held nothing back on the story. Dobber and Shelby Snyder were dispatched to Carrollton and Radcliff—Dobber to chronicle the awful end, Snyder to tell the stories of those who died. Inside the office, Carson drew the assignment that simultaneously framed his larger future at the *Argus-Dispatch* and challenged his inner sense of being able to handle it. Reardon charged him with shepherding all of the coverage—and there would be endless reams of it, from the safety standards of buses in Kentucky to the burn rate of foam seating to the fortification of drunken-driving laws.

Hector sits up and nuzzles Carson's arm, wanting more attention. Carson strokes his back, the fingers digging deep into Hector's fur, and the dog settles into the passenger seat.

Two memories bubble up that Carson has never been able to shake, the kind that come on randomly at night and leave him blinking into the darkness. The first, from Dobber's initial day on the ground in Carrollton, was a matter of grim accounting. After the survivors were treated and taken away and the fire was put out, the Kentucky State Police loaded the bus onto a flatbed and took it to the National Guard armory. There, out of sight of the gawkers, officers moved through the seats, finding and removing the bodies. Dobber's source, a cop he had known back in high school, told him that many of the dead had been found facing the rear exit, the only one available to them after the wall of flames began moving in from the front. They knew they had to get out and they couldn't, and they died there, just feet away from deliverance. Carson shook that one off outside the *Argus-Dispatch* building, holding a bummed cigarette in his shaky fingers as he took a walk alone.

A week later, Carson stood in the composing room, giving one last look to a doubletruck spread of vignettes about the victims. As he reconciled names and ages—so many lives gone so soon and forever—he broke down, setting his head against the pasted-up pages. Most of his colleagues inched away—perhaps out of deference but mostly out of fear, Carson suspected. They had all been subsisting on caffeine and nicotine for days, and emotions were frayed, and nobody wanted to show public grief or humanness. Carson felt shame at letting it all get to him.

Only Reardon acknowledged the moment, sliding an arm across Carson's shoulders and pulling him in. "You're going to run this place someday," he said. In the years that followed, that prophetic utterance had been the source of considerable angst. Carson went home that night and did a fist pump in his living room, an act that quickly yielded to guilt. In one breath, he wondered how he could build a career on the foundation of such enormity. In the next, he tortured himself by refusing to be selfless. A better man would say that he would trade it all to bring those kids back, a futile bargaining with a fate that had already played out. Carson knew he wouldn't. And he knew that the inevitable question about God's role in such calamity— *what loving God could allow this to happen?*—led him to the same conclusion he had already reached years earlier, one he told his mother the day after his daddy died, one that broke her heart: There is no God. The universe shakes us all out at random, which is how a drunken factory worker and a bunch of good-hearted kids can end up at the same place at the same horrific moment. It's all chance, and chance is a son of a bitch.

"I'm getting out," Carson says, and Hector, a permissive dog, sits up to watch him go and then settles back down onto his haunches as Carson waits for a cluster of cars to pass like a school of fish on the current. The crossing clear, Carson walks to the median strip, headed for the crosses and wilted flowers.

The man who killed all those kids is on Carson's mind now. It's never been lost on Carson that he and the pickup driver probably found out about the crash around the same time. The driver was told the next day, after he woke up in a hospital bed with no recollection of what had happened, no knowledge of the terror he had unleashed, of kids dying in two-thousand-degree heat. How does one even deal with a moment like that, or every moment that follows? By the time sentencing came and the guy received sixteen years, there was no penalty that would have satisfied some people. Over the years, though, Carson has developed a grudging tolerance for the man. Part of it, he believes, lies in the survivors' attitudes, a display of Christian values that Carson so rarely sees in Christians anymore: By and large, they've offered forgiveness. The rest of Carson's uneasy acceptance of his existence has been shaped by how the story keeps coming back. In five year waves—1993, 1998, 2003, 2008—the event returns to prominence in mid-May, and newspapers and television stations tap their archives and send reporters out to find some new way of telling an old story. Those efforts invariably would involve the driver, who never said a word, never responded to an interview request. Now out of prison longer than he'd ever been in, he's a ghost who lives not far from where Carson now stands. He's had the good sense—perhaps even the respect—to keep to himself.

Carson fingers a faded ribbon holding together the sun-baked husks of twenty-seven roses and wonders what the man thinks when he passes this site, if he can bring himself to do it. Is he tortured all over again, or has he buried it deep, like shrapnel encased in scar tissue? The answer isn't likely to come. The man who did this marks his time and his deeds in isolation and silence, and Carson thinks he can understand that. It's probably the only way.

At the car, Hector pokes his head up from the seat and barks at Carson.

"In a minute."

Hector barks again.

"OK, dammit."

Carson lets the ribbon go and watches it flap in the breeze. He takes one last sweeping view of the site, and then he closes his eyes, as if to brand it on his brain. He wants to remember this, all of it. The curve of the road and the hand-delivered memorials and the rocky hillside right there where the bus burned. When he comes through Monday, he intends to drive past that sign with all due speed, to not even look at it if he can help doing so, and continue on to Louisville and his appointment with Dan Dempsey. And then, he swears, he will never pass this way again.

November 11, 2013

Dear Cara ...

Thank you for the letter and the pictures.

Pictures first: It's all way beyond my pay grade, or what was my pay grade, but how cool that you can actually show me how the antibodies recognize insulin and go fluorescent like that. It's wild to think of how things work on a cellular level, how completely mind-boggling it is that so many processes are at work in so infinitesimally small a place, and seeing it was really cool. Thank you. You're doing important work on behalf of fatasses like me. (Although I should note that I'm no longer quite so fat: down ninety pounds, thanks to a reduced appetite and plenty of time to do that exercise I always disdained.)

As for the letter, I want you to know how much I appreciate your sharing your thoughts about faith. I have a long way to go before I'm where you are on the whole God question, but I think I'm starting to appreciate how you can divide your life in the lab, where everything has a measurement, and your belief in God. Seems to me that without that division, you'd be in constant conflict. And, of course, I envy your peace with such a conflict. I hope we can keep talking about this.

I've definitely been thinking about it. Your example about how love can't be proved and yet we don't doubt it when we have it really hit home with me. I've been coming up with similar examples. For instance, one day I'm going to try to make the case that I'm ready to get on with it. I won't be able to prove it, per se, but I'll do my best to demonstrate it. And then I'm going to have to hope someone has faith in me.

It's been a long time since I've had that hope. It feels good.

Thanks again, for everything ...
Carson

Saturday, Afternoon

Carson gives up. He has ambled from building to building to building on this campus dropped in a low-rent section of Cincinnati, where the sidewalks are choked with weeds and there's a car repair place on every corner, and Dr. Cara Echols—doctor!—can't be found because the doors won't open. He fades back to the parking lot and settles into the driver's seat.

Hector, beaten down by the ride and the advancing heat, licks Carson's hand.

"I know, boy."

Hector slips his snout between Carson's arm and the center console.

"I know. I can't find her."

Hector grumbles and adjusts in the bucket seat.

The calendar occurs to Carson. "Oh, shit. It's Saturday, isn't it?" He never lost track when he was working.

The dog sneezes.

"OK, I'm going."

At a gas station two blocks up, Carson finds the last phone booth in America and, in a bonus, a full directory in it. He wastes two quarters on listings for C. Echols that most assuredly are not Cara. *The whole damn world has a cellphone.* At last, he calls the University of Cincinnati switchboard and listens to the Muzak version of "Sister Golden Hair" circulate in his ear as the automated attendant engages the connecting number. With his free hand, Carson grips himself around the throat and pulls his thumb and forefinger together, catching the grime between them. He lifts his fingers. The onion rings from lunch, seasoned with a day's sweat, linger on his nose.

"Dr. Cara Echols."

"Cara!"

"This is Dr. Cara Echols."

"I'm so glad you're there. This is Dr. Carson McCullough, Ph.D. in good times!" Carson winces.

"Carson?"

"The one and only."

"Wow. I mean—wow. This is unexpected."

"But welcome, right?" *You fucking apple polisher, insecure asshole.*

"Yes, of course. It's so good to hear from you."

"Let me ask you something. Where are you?"

"I'm—I'm at work, Carson. You called me."

He stamps his foot and grimaces. "What I mean is, where is that? I came by the building there on East Galbraith, and it was all locked up. That place is a damn maze."

"Wait, you're here? Like, right here?"

"Surprise!"

"Wow. OK, you're here now?"

"No, now I'm at a gas station. But I can be there soon."

A smidge of silence enters the conversation. "If you want," he throws in.

"No. I mean—yes, of course. Of course. Come back and walk to the door of the front building. I'll meet you in the lobby."

"OK. I'll be the one with the flowers. You know, it's been a while. You might not recognize me."

"I think I will."

"It's no big deal. I got them at Meijer. You like carnations, right? I think I remember that."

"Yes, of course."

"It's just a little gesture from a friend you haven't seen in a long time."

"Carson, hang up the phone and drive over here."

"Right. Be there in a jiff."

Carson returns the phone to the cradle, turns and heads back to the car, head hung low, making the perp walk of the eternally uncool. Hector waits, unimpressed.

She's as lovely as she was the day she left, only more so, if that's even possible. The hair is close-cropped now and off her shoulders, and threads of gray run through it, but the face...*oh, God, the face.* That smile and gentle approachability that had Carson burning ruts in the floor as he wheeled his chair closer to hers all those years ago, it's all still there, and Carson's heart and his stomach meet in the middle of his chest as she pushes open the door and lets him in.

"For you," he says, crashing the flowers into her shoulder as she leans in for a half-hug.

"I'm sorry," he says.

She pats his free elbow. "This is such a surprise. You look— you look good, Carson."

He slides his hand over his shirt, feeling the contour of his ample belly, touching down to the front of his jeans where he surreptitiously checks his fly. She's being nice. He knows how he looks—about eighty-five pounds heavier than when she last saw him. And here they stand in a place where she researches obesity. That's some cruel poetry.

He pushes the flowers forward again, and she takes them. "You didn't have to."

"I wanted to see you."

She does a little curtsy. "Here I am."

"Here you are."

She gathers herself. "I wish I'd known you were coming."

"That would have ruined the surprise."

"Ah, yes. Listen, do you want—do you want to come up to my office and talk for a bit. I'm afraid I don't have much time. I'm prepping for this conference—"

"Actually, can I get some water? Hector's pretty thirsty."

"Hector?"

"Yeah, you remember my dog." *You remember my heart, right, Cara? You remember how you just up and left and that was it except for three Christmas cards, right? You remember?*

"Hector's here?"

"Outside in the car."

She holds her hands to her face and claps twice in quick succession. "Can I see him?"

"He'll be pissed off if you don't." She smiles, a real, fulsome smile, her first, and says she has a bottle of water upstairs and she'll go get it and she'll be right back and wait here for just a second, OK?

"OK."

He watches her turn and jog away toward the stairs, angles and curves in perfect proportion, an enviable surety to every movement, and he's smitten all again, as he knew he would be.

Hector sits in the seat, paws overhanging, and laps water from a foam cup that Cara offers as she kneels before him. The whole thing looks entirely too regal to Carson.

"He's worn out, the poor guy," she says.

"He ought to be. Damn showoff." It was the damnedest thing, Hector's reaction to Cara. He bounded out of the car and ran to her upon hearing her voice, throwing his front paws onto her hips in an approximation of a hug. She led him to the greenbelt and gave him a good scratching. He flopped onto his back and wriggled for her, and she stroked his tummy and bent in close for kisses, and Carson just stood there on the asphalt, watching in wonderment as Hector tried to roll back his years. All for a woman. All things Carson would have done given the same opportunity.

"He's not a showoff," she says, her words baby talk. "He's a good boy." Hector, wet-mouthed, kisses her again. It's perfectly ridiculous.

Carson slips his hands into his back pockets and rocks back on his heels. "That good boy has been a pain in the butt for two days now. But he told me he wanted to see you, so here we are."

She cups the dog's cheeks in her hands and rubs them in swirls. Hector, entranced, goes wherever she wants to lead him. "That's funny," she says. "But, really, you just up and came to Cincinnati?"

"We made a few stops. A few inquiries about jobs."

"Anything promising?"

Carson doesn't speak until she looks up at him. "No."

"Something will turn." And there she is again. Sensible Cara. He remembers sitting with her as she made the reveal about leaving the *Argus-Dispatch*, how dispassionate so much of it seemed. He'd reached for her hands, and she gave him a single clasp and then let go. She kept latching on to neutral language, about how it would all work out for both of them, and he kept dying invisibly across from her. It's the same thing now. He wants to hear sympathy or empathetic anger, but no, it's "something will turn."

"I'm talking to Dempsey at the *Times* in a couple of days.

Might be something there. You remember him, don't you?"

"I don't think so."

"I'm sure we did something one time with him and his wife. Waterskiing, wasn't it? You sure you don't remember?"

"It was a long time ago."

"It doesn't seem like it sometimes."

Cara turns back to Hector. Carson walks to the driver's side of the car and opens the door. He reaches in and scratches the ridgeline of Hector's back.

"What else are you doing while you're here?" she asks.

"Hanging out with you."

"No, seriously."

"I'm serious as can be."

Cara isn't looking at him. It's not that she isn't looking at him that bothers Carson. It's that she's trying not to look at him.

"That's—that's not possible, Carson. I'm sorry. I wish you'd called. I have so much to do. I'm flying to Zurich Monday—"

"Come on, it's Saturday. Are you kidding? Work?"

"Like I said, I have this—"

"Have dinner with me."

Cara looks up.

"With us," he says.

"I can't."

"Come on, one dinner. We'll go quietly after that. We've barely had time to talk."

"I shouldn't."

"Come on."

She looks back over her shoulder, at her building and the attendant work just a few strides away. Carson follows her eyes, and an unreasonable thought inhabits his head. If she goes for the front door, he's going to have to run his fat ass and get in front of her. That's the extent of the plan, which leaves a considerable number of gaps.

She kisses Hector on the nose. "For the chance to hang out with this sweet boy, how could I say no?"

Carson slides into the driver's seat.

"Get in," he says. "Hector, in the back."

Hector, a dog accustomed to riding in the front, throws a sulky look over his shoulder. Carson jerks a thumb. "In back." Hector at last complies.

Cara drops into the passenger seat, a poof of fine dog dander rising into the air.

"Ready?" Carson asks.

"As I'll ever be."

Carson whips the Mustang around and points it toward the road. Hector's bandanna leaves his neck and floats down, down, down on the draft, settling atop a hedge. Nobody notices. They're gone.

Saturday, Dusk

"I never eat this. I mean, never." Cara opens wide to fit the chili-cheese coney from Skyline into her mouth. As she chews, she closes her eyes in fast-food nirvana. "And this is why," she says at last. "*Sooo* good. If I start, I'll weigh two hundred pounds."

Carson sets his bowl of three-way spaghetti down and runs his hands along the topography of his gut. He picks the food up again and eats.

"Hector!" he shouts. The dog, turned loose in the small corner park, has unearthed a dead bird. He drops it and moves away as if to plead *I'm just picking up around here, no problem, don't worry about it, boss.*

"What else have you been doing on your trip?" Cara asks. She's perched on the Mustang's hood, her legs stretched out before her. Carson, afraid to crawl all the way onto the car, leans against the front of it.

"No sightseeing. Just looking for a job. Gotta do something. Too young to retire." His face turns stormy.

"What?" she asks.

"Do you remember the Carrollton bus crash?"

"Yes. Yes, of course."

"I was at the site today. First time."

"You've never been there?"

"No." He twirls spaghetti on his fork, lifts it toward his mouth and then sets it back down. He fastens the plastic lid over the takeout bowl. "I never wanted to see it. Always went out of my way to avoid it."

Cara, too, discards her food. Hector lifts a leg on a birch.

"You know, what happened that night is pretty much the reason I ended up with the job I had," he says at last.

"I didn't know that," she says. "I was in high school when it happened. I've seen the sign, though."

"I hate that sign. I wish they'd take it down."

"Why?"

"Who wants to—you know what? It doesn't matter. I'm sorry. I didn't come here to bum you out. Tell me about what's going on with you. What's this about Zurich?"

She sets a hand on his and then pulls it back. "I'd rather talk about this."

"No."

"Maybe it'll make you feel better."

"About what?" He says it loud and with anger, and she flinches and shows a flash of fear, and then it's over and she's back to implacable, that eternal poker face that always made him wonder what she was really thinking. *Did she love him back then?* The words were always in reserve with him, ready for an excuse to be unwrapped. She never gave him one.

"God, Cara. I hope you never get to a place in your life where you wonder if that's all there is."

"What do you mean?"

"I've squandered it, don't you get it? I should have done what you did, got out, did something else with my life, something that meant something." He bites off what he wants to say next, about how his life's work was for nothing and nobody, that it can just end one day and nobody cares. He hates the idea of this kind of cheapo self-help, sitting-on-Dr.-Phil's-couch sort of talk tumbling from his mouth.

"Come on. I'll admit, the newsroom wasn't for me, but Carson, come on. You belonged there. You were never so happy as when you were at work. Don't second-guess that just because the paper got shut down."

Carson stares at the ground, at a single piece of agate stuck halfway under the toe of his shoe, a rock different from every other rock he can see—it's pink and purple and orange and shades in between. Carson thinks of the worlds folded into this one, of single molecules in the rock that hold their own tiny universes, and he thinks that he's never felt more insignificant.

"I don't know how to do anything else. I don't want to do anything else."

"I know," she says.

He laughs, rueful. "I'd scream at God if I believed in him."

Hector wanders over, drawn by the escalating and fading talk. He stands before them, his head moving from Carson to Cara and back again, expectant. Cara slides off the front of the car and scrunches down to Hector's eye level and scratches his ears.

"I believe in God," she says.

"Right."

"I'm serious."

"Hector, come here." The dog gives no sign of hearing Carson, who redirects his attention. "Well, that's a surprise."

"How? I've always believed in God."

Carson is off the car now and several feet away from Cara and Hector. "I figured the line of work you're in would have disproved those notions by now."

She stands up and shoos Hector toward Carson. Hector holds his ground. "I'm a researcher, not a clearinghouse for the existence of God."

"I know. It's just—"

"Besides that, science doesn't set out to disprove the existence of anything. We're interested in what we can discover, not what we can't."

"So you can't prove God exists?"

"Of course not. Nobody can." She climbs back atop the hood and pats it, inviting him to join her. Head down, he returns to the car.

"So you believe all that earth-was-created-in-six-days stuff?"

"You're talking about the Bible, Carson, and religion. I didn't say I believe in that. I said I believe in God."

"Are you a Christian?"

"Yes."

"Isn't the Bible the basis of your faith, then?"

She sweeps her hand across the side of her head, tucking her hair behind her ear. Carson looks closer and sees tiny wrinkles where her jaw meets her earlobe. *It's been a long time.*

"My faith is more interior than that, and more driven by what I see in the world and what I feel in my bones," she says.

"So you don't believe in evolution?"

"Carson, nobody who has ever looked into a genome denies evolution. Natural selection happened. It is happening. That's a matter of fact, not belief. But I'll tell you something: Looking into a genome fortifies my faith. Learning all of the functions a single cell has to do precisely right, every time, in order to sustain life, that fortifies my faith. It's hard for me to look at these things and not come to the conclusion that this was the design of a force I can't begin to fully understand. In that, I see God."

Carson turns toward her. She's heading now into the territory that has challenged his thoughts off and on since his daddy fell to the linoleum. "But doesn't it drive you crazy to not know? I'm not even a scientist, and that makes me nuts. My mom and dad, they used to be on my ass all the time to go to church, to believe. As long as I was in their house, I did, but as soon as I got out, man, I started thinking for myself. Like today. I'm sitting there where all those kids burned up, and I'm thinking, what kind of loving God lets that happen? What's the fucking plan in that?"

She speaks in calm proportional to his anger. "Maybe there isn't one."

"Right. That's what I'm saying. Because if God loves us, what possible greater good is there in that? There's not any. When my dad died, I went outside our house and I screamed at the sky. Where was God in that? When my mom died, shit, I didn't even bother. You know why? Because it's a waste of breath to talk to God when he's not there."

"Are you sure God's not there?" she asks.

"Are you sure he is?"

"That's not my question. I have faith that he—or something— is. That's what faith is: the act of believing in something that cannot be proved to you."

Carson gets back on his feet and goes around to the driver's side. He drops into the seat and turns on the radio. The station he found as he drove into Cincinnati blasts forth.

"You know this song?" he asks over the windshield.

" 'Centerfold.' Sure."

"But this isn't the J. Geils Band."

"It isn't?"

"No. You see, the way my car radio works is there's this little rock band that lives inside it. These guys are small but totally awesome. They can play every song ever written, and they can make it sound just like the original artist."

"Interesting."

"But here's the thing," he says. "If you dismantle the radio, these guys disappear. If you put a camera in there, they don't show up on the film. Now, do you believe that shit?"

She turns herself around on the hood of the car. "No."

"Why not?"

"Well, I know how radios work, how receivers—"

"Not this radio."

"OK, but I just heard the station's call letters, and it's a signal here in Cincinnati, so everything I can gather about the situation leads me to the conclusion that this radio works the same as every other radio."

"But it doesn't."

"If you say so."

"How sure are you of your position?" he asks her.

"As sure as I need to be."

"Are you one hundred percent sure?"

"I'm ninety-nine-point-nine percent sure."

"Why not one hundred percent?"

"Because I can't disprove what you say. Don't you see? You're making my point. Now let me ask you this: Do you really believe there's a little rock band inside your radio?"

"Hector!" The dog, caught nosing through a pile of garbage, hangs his head and comes to the car. The movements are painful for Carson to watch, as seemingly a dozen parts of Hector's body sway independent of each other and in all the wrong directions.

"Do you?" she asks.

Carson steps out and lets Hector clamber into the back.

"As much as I believe in God, yeah."

Silent panic stirs in Carson's chest, rising to his throat. As Cara's office building comes into view, so too does the inevitable goodbye.

"I wish we had more time," he says.

"Yeah, this has been fun. What are you going to do now?"

"The Reds are in town. Maybe see a game. No, wait, shit, I can't. Not with Hector. I'll find something to do. Go back Monday, see Dan, see what comes of that."

"And if that doesn't work out?"

"I guess I'll work at Haller's museum."

"Will that be so bad?"

Carson pulls into the parking lot. He doesn't want to answer. "Hang out with us tomorrow."

She shakes her head. "I can't."

"You don't leave till Monday, you said."

"Yeah, but Carson, I have so much work to do before then."

He turns in the seat and faces her. "Come on."

"I can't."

"I was really nervous about seeing you, Cara."

She clasps her hands in front of her. "I was surprised. But I'm glad you came."

"I've been thinking about a lot of things lately, especially with all that's happened. A lot of things I wish maybe I'd done differently."

"Like what?" She looks at him.

"Did you love me?"

She takes the question without blinking. "I don't know."

"I was waiting for the right time to say it," he says. "Or maybe I was waiting for you to say it first. And then you were gone. I always wonder, what if I hadn't been so chickenshit—"

"Carson, no, don't. I think I could have loved you. But something came up, you know? That's life."

He leans across the console to kiss her, fast so he doesn't think better of it, this plan he's had half-hatched since he and Hector crossed the Ohio River the first time. Kiss her, and it will all work out somehow.

Her right hand, erect, stops him. "No. I don't want this."

Hector whines from the back seat. Carson slumps back and tries to press his body through the door to get away from her. "I thought you did."

She reaches for the door handle. "I didn't mean—I didn't think—I didn't intend to send that message."

"You said you wished it had ended differently."

"What?"

"In your email."

"I—" With shaky fingers, she picks up her purse. "My email?"

"'I wish it could have ended differently than it did.' That's what you said." He doesn't look at her.

"Oh, God, Carson, I meant your job at the *Argus-Dispatch*. I wish it could have ended differently. Not you and me." He flinches at the final four words, and she reaches to touch his elbow in reassurance. He pulls back, out of reach.

"I'm going to go," she says. "I'm sorry about this. I think it's best that I go."

She's out of the door when he says, "Wait, Cara." She turns back, her face red.

"Are you involved with someone?" he asks.

"Yes."

"Someone you'll see in Zurich?"

She slides a finger across her lips. "Yes."

He starts the Mustang. As he backs up and out, she catches the door and closes it. He stops and then puts the car in drive. She walks toward him. "Carson—"

He lays a long track of rubber down as he burns the tires and rides past her, out the gate and onto the road.

Saturday, Evening

The road bends like an elbow at Florence, Kentucky. Carson's headlights nick the man standing there, far too close to the white line. He stands beneath the overpass and holds his sign aloft in hope, the letters jeweled like a teenage girl's jeans bottoms: GOING WHEREVER YOU ARE.

Carson eases the Mustang to the shoulder, and he watches through the rearview as the man tucks his sign under an arm and clomps over. His tall, bony body moves out of rhythm, and his long, stringy, salt-and-pepper hair sprouts from a trucker's cap.

"In the back," Carson says to Hector, jerking a thumb rearward. Hector slides across the console and sits in a huff.

The highway man opens the passenger door and ducks his head in. "Thank you, kindest sir." Carson sizes him up. Six-four, maybe six-five. Thin. Can't be more than a middleweight. Doesn't smell like ass.

"Where you headed?" Carson asks.

"Going wherever you are." The man taps his sign twice.

"So you said. Get in."

T he miles fall away in a soliloquy.

"See, the thing was, I knew when I met Sonya—she was my jezebel, I told you that, yes?—I knew I would fall. I am not a strong man, no sir, I am not, and when I met Sonya, I knew I was not strong enough to stay away from her. I tried, Lord yes, I tried. But I fell. I knew I would."

The highway man gave his name as Jagur, which Carson figures to be the fakest name ever, but who cares? Carson introduced himself as Jimmy Joe Ray Bob Dale—"honest to goodness," he said—and faked out the faker. Jagur sits in the passenger seat and dangles a hand into the backseat of the car, stroking Hector's undercoat and sending the dog into contented sleep.

"Wait," Carson says. " 'Fell'? So does that mean you boinked this Sonya chick?"

"An unnecessarily crude assessment, I rather think, but yes, that is what happened."

"So what?"

"She was not mine to boink, as you so colorfully put it. I am a married man. I have a daughter who is on the student council and the Honor Society. I should have no time for jezebels. It was a sin."

"So what are you doing out here? Go home. Be with your family. Forget Sonya. A mistake."

Jagur's hand leaves Hector and palms the dashboard. The hand is massive, vascular. He sweeps it across the dash, leaving a grooved trail of dust.

"Are you married, Mr. Ray Bob Dale?"

"That's Mr. Dale. The rest is my first name."

"My apologies. Are you married?"

"No."

"Ever married?"

"No."

Jagur again massages Hector. "Forget Sonya, you say. I could sooner forget a knife plunged into my heart. God is testing me, Mr. Dale. When I told my wife—"

"You told your wife?"

"I am not a keeper of secrets, Mr. Dale. When I told my wife, she and God said that I should leave the house and venture into the world. The truth of the matter is that my wife said only that I should leave the house. It was God's idea that I go into the world. My penance is out here. My test is out here. And when I have passed it, when I have satisfied God, I shall return again to my wife and to my daughter and to the world I am not presently fit to live in."

The words land in Carson's ears with a softness that is, at once, eerie and intoxicating. The guy is whacked out of his ever-loving gourd. Of that, Carson is sure. He's seen guys like Jagur, the modern-day drifters, the ones who would stop at the *Argus-Dispatch* and ask to speak with the editor and would show him close-up photographs of the trees and would ask Carson if he could see the eyes that haunted them———the CIA, they claimed, or maybe special-ops soldiers. Carson never could, and he would offer the men a vending-machine sandwich and directions to the crisis center. Those men, he suspected, knew they were crazy. But Jagur—Jagur has no idea.

Carson turns down the radio. "What do you mean, into the world?"

"Those very words and none other, Mr. Dale. I go wherever I am meant to go, and what happens to me is what I'm meant to endure. If young men wish to beat me, to steal from me, I take it and then I thank God and then I move on. If I'm meant to sleep in a gutter, that is where I rest my head."

"You've been beaten up?"

"Many, many times. But not enough. Not yet."

Carson looks to his right, and he's met by penetrating eyes—

the kind that know pain, hunger, desperation. The kind that neither move nor threaten.

"How do you know this is what God wants?" Carson asks.

"God makes himself clear to those who listen."

"That's not really an answer, though."

"Mr. Dale, do you listen to God?"

"Yes." This is a lie. "But I wouldn't presume to speak for him." This is the truth.

"I am not speaking for him," Jagur says. "Only obeying."

"So what if God told you to blow up a building?"

Jagur looks stricken. "A man who listens to God hears no such counsel. A man who hurts others in the name of God is perverting God for his own purposes."

Carson taps the steering wheel twice. "But isn't that what you're doing anyway? I mean, no disrespect, Mr. Jagur, but—"

"Just Jagur, Mr. Dale. This is not my surname."

"OK, but isn't it convenient to say, 'Look, I had no say in the matter. I had to boink this Sonya chick, and now I have to go into the world as my penance'? Just go home, man. Be a good husband. Be a good father. Leave God out of it."

Jagur doesn't answer, not for a long stretch. Carson grips the steering wheel.

"I like you, Mr. Dale. You are a good debater. Of course, the idea of leaving God out of it holds no currency, but I suspect you know this. You and I may quibble over whether I accepted or rejected self-determinism with regard to my jezebel. But the matter of God's role is not open to interpretation. One of us is simply misguided. I feel confident in my position."

"And I in mine. And, look, I like you, too, Jagur," Carson says. He looks at the cardboard riding on Jagur's knees. "I really like your sign."

The grim face breaks. Jagur smiles and turns the cardboard around so the letters show to Carson. "My sign gathers attention.

It is a necessity. I have no wish to be flashy, Mr. Dale, but it is flashiness in the service of truth. I'm going where you're going."

Carson's laugh is bitter, acidic. "You're better off going the other way."

"There is no other way."

"I'm just saying."

"As am I."

Carson locks his elbows as he grips the wheel. "Right, so we've exhausted that. It sounds kind of grotesque, this journey of yours."

"If that is your conclusion, I have no standing to argue."

"Why take the beatings? Why not fight for what you want?"

"Taking the beatings is my fight."

"So when do you know it's over?"

"When I am home."

"And where is that?"

Jagur holds a finger, laced with scar tissue, to his lips. "It would not be sporting to tell you, as you could decide to take me there."

"That would be a bad thing?"

"That would not be God's will. I am going where you're going. Someday, someone will be going to my home."

Ahead, the lights of a town guide the Mustang in. Carson checks the gas gauge and sees it wanting.

"Well, Jagur, I'm going to La Grange."

"As am I."

"Is that home?"

Again, Jagur crosses his lips with his finger. "It would not be sporting to tell you."

From the Louisville Times, Sunday, April 22, 2012:

The abrupt closure last week of a well-regarded western Kentucky newspaper seemed to catch readers and advertisers by surprise, but veteran industry watchers say such a move has been coming for a long time, driven by an aging readership, a collapse in all-important classified advertising and a technological environment bending toward digital news delivery.

"I guess the shock, in this case, was that it came in an isolated market, at a smaller newspaper, and those have generally performed better than their larger metropolitan counterparts," said David Trucks, who covers the industry for *The New York Times*. "But in a vacuum, the idea of a newspaper closing its doors isn't shocking at all. Indeed, I'd say that we should prepare ourselves to hear this story much more often."

Newspaper companies have long hoped that the ascendency of online news delivery, and the dollars associated with it, would eventually replace the revenue generated by the print product, and that, combined with the savings associated with the elimination of printing presses and costly home delivery, would eventually make online newsgathering viable financially. That turned out to not be the case at the *Argus-Dispatch*, and it's not happening in many other places, either, Trucks said.

"A lot of these companies are in a real bind," he said. "In many cases, they have massive debt to service, so they need not just a healthy margin, but a lot of money—and print still pays the biggest share of the freight. They're finding it difficult to move toward online and maintain the newsroom staffing necessary to cover their communities. This is a customer service issue and, I'd argue, a democracy issue. Who's going to mind the public till if newspapers go away? A good newspaper isn't just the source of basic, commodity news. It binds a community together and keeps it civilized."

Sunday, Early Morning

Dan Dempsey stands on the downslope of his front yard, in canvas shorts and a fraying Kentucky Wildcats T-shirt, and regards Carson, who has a line of caked blood running from the nostrils of his smashed nose to the pocket of his shirt.

"Jesus Christ, man. What the hell happened to you?"

"You wouldn't believe me if I told you. We gotta talk." Carson's words come out nasal and clipped, a predictable if unfortunate byproduct of hammering one's own nose with a tire iron. The hell of it is, Carson had intended to do much worse as he stood in the dim light of the gas station bathroom outside La Grange. His intention had been to beat himself into submission, a notion half ignited by that lilting lunatic Jagur. As the first swing bore down, Carson thought better of it—*because you're a fucking pussy*—and couldn't pull back the iron in time. He stumbled back out to Hector, light-headed and incoherent as if he'd been chomping oxycontin.

He stares at Dempsey, who keeps his distance. "OK, talk."

"Can we go inside? Jesus, Dan, I could use an aspirin and some coffee."

"Maybe."

"Maybe?"

"My kids are in there, Carson. You're a mess. Talk to me, and we'll see."

Carson traces a path along the edge of the lawn, up from the mailbox to the contoured driveway and the hedges that look perpetually maintained. The house, a sandy-colored brick rambler, nestles into a tiered front yard. "Nice place. Jeffersontown, man. You've really done well for yourself."

"Thank you." As Carson moves, he sees Dempsey hold his place save for pivots to keep his college chum in his sights. Carson, spotting this, opts to moves left and right, turning Dempsey into a metronome.

"So, you talk to me, Dan," he says. "You're the one who wanted to talk."

"We're supposed to do that tomorrow, as I recall. Downtown. In my office."

"No can do, Dan. I'm going back home today."

Dempsey looks to the front door and sees his wife through the side window. He holds up a hand. *It's OK.*

"It's about this position I have open."

Carson walks down the slope to him. "Yeah?"

"OK, this sounds silly, but we gave it kind of a superhero name: mobile action reporter. Basically, it's a multiplatform thing, somebody who gets dispatched wherever we need him and files to the blog, to the breaking-news part of the website, shoots video and has the depth to write quick reads and, occasionally, some deeper stories. This is somebody who's going to live in a car and who eats and breathes news."

"That sounds awesome, man. What a great idea." Carson expels the words in an excited jumble.

"I'm glad you think so. It's a pretty bold idea, at least for us, and it's going to take somebody with a particularly broad set of skills to do the job right."

"Of course. Yes. Yes! So many possibilities in a job like that."

"Right. So, anyway, the reason I wanted to talk to you about it is this guy, Timmy Bardo, applied last week."

"Wait." Carson swallows hard and steadies himself. Pockets of air float through his chest, and he wonders if he's going to pass out. "Bardo?"

"Yeah, he listed you as a reference. Is this guy any good? He sure looks good on paper."

"Bardo." Carson turns away from Dempsey and heads back toward the driveway. "Yeah, Bardo's good. Young. A work in progress." He laughs—not gently like he sounds in his own head, but loud and maniacal. "But then, Dan, I guess we all are."

"Can he do this job?"

Carson turns again and walks at double speed down the hill toward his friend. Dempsey sets himself. "He's a good kid, Dan, but he's not right for this job."

"No?"

"No. Come on, man, you're reinventing the wheel here. You need somebody who knows what the wheel looks like."

Dempsey shakes his head. "I'm confused. Bardo included his last performance review in his package. You wrote it. You said 'Timmy can do anything he wants to do in this business.' I mean, Christ, the whole reason I'm talking to you is because of that."

"Dan, I could do that job for you. I could do it like nobody's business. You know me. You know this about me."

Dempsey backs up a few steps. "Carson, I—what? Man, you don't even own a cell phone."

"That's doesn't mean I don't know how the goddamn things work." He advances on Dempsey, who puts up his fists.

"Carson, go home. You're better than this."

"I want the job, Dan."

"Yeah, well, you're not getting it. Don't be ridiculous. You don't want this. You just want something, because something's been taken from you. Well, tough shit, pal. Welcome to the big, bad world."

Carson moves in, and Dempsey shoves him back, and Carson cuts down the distance again. "Easy for you to say. Nice fucking house, Dan. Nice fucking family. I bet you got a nice fucking mortgage, and soon you'll have a nice fucking coronary, you fraud."

Carson's hot breath, redolent of the blood he's swallowed, crashes into Dempsey, who backpedals to the front door. "Go home. I'm serious, Carson. Get out of here or I'm calling the cops." Dempsey opens the door and backs into the house. The door closes, and he watches Carson from the window.

Carson stands defiant in the yard. With the back of his hand, he clears a fresh batch of snot and blood from his nose, his eyes never leaving Dempsey's.

Behind him, in the car, Hector stirs, bolting up in the seat. He spots Carson and barks.

Carson stands his ground. He points a shaking finger toward the house. "You owe me this, Dan."

Hector barks again.

Carson watches through the window as Dempsey punches numbers into a phone.

Carson turns and walks away.

"OK, boy, I'm coming."

Sunday, Getaway Day

Super Valu Saver, South Hurstbourne Parkway, Louisville

It's at his second stop after Dempsey's house that Carson figures out how it's going to go down. At the first Super Valu he visited, on Bashford Manor Lane, it was mostly legit: He went to the men's clothing section and told the friendly young woman there—Rita—that he had been hit in the nose by a foul ball and needed to clean up and buy a new shirt. While she fussed over him and went off in search of his size and preferred style ("Collared, short sleeves, please"), he slipped a three-pack of tube socks down his pants. Rita, all of nineteen and naive enough to believe his lies, let him scrub down in the employee bathroom and wear the shirt out the door, after he paid for it, of course, which was the least he could do.

Now, on South Hurstbourne, Carson drives through the parking lot to the back of the store. A green Mustang—one with a dog as a copilot—isn't the most inauspicious vehicle in the world, so Carson figures he's going to have to take a different tack. He parks the car at the back door and tells Hector to stay, and Hector, a dog who understands the value of obedience in the commission of shoplifting, lies down in the front seat.

Carson gets out and jiggles the door handle, and damned if it doesn't open. Lax security protocols at a store famous for putting the pinch on would-be thieves isn't something he counted on, but he'll take any advantage he can. He slips into the darkened storeroom and waits for his eyes to adjust.

The first two steps Carson takes echo off the polished concrete floor. He stops. He kicks off his shoes, one at a time, left and then right. He carries the shoes to the door, opens it and tosses them into the back seat. Hector, roused, pokes up his head.

"Stay," Carson whispers. Hector recedes into the seat.

Back inside the storeroom, Carson assesses the layout. His luck remains strong. In front of him sits a pallet of twenty-two-inch flat-screen TVs. He steps forward.

After leaving Dempsey's house, Carson had driven in random loops around the neighborhood, trying to figure out what to do next. The limits of choice (go home or stay here or be stupid) and funding (seriously, cash is low and it's time to go home) struck him as profoundly unsatisfying, and a lifetime of taking the conventional options had brought him here, so Carson McCullough had made a definitive if not defined decision: *the hell with it all.*

That ethos, by its nature, leaves details and goals fuzzy. Carson grabs a boxed TV set and heads for the exit in his stocking feet. Had it been a pallet of boxed macaroni dinners, he'd have grabbed a case. Bottled water, the same. Women's underwear. Shampoo. Garden gnomes. It doesn't matter.

He puts the TV in the back seat next to the socks. "Good boy," he says to Hector, who sniffs the merchandise.

As the Mustang tears out of there, the security camera fastened to the top of the store, the one focused on the area in front of the door, continues to roll. Three cameras inside the storeroom already have Carson's image. So does the one in the menswear department on Bashford Manor Lane. When the security division reconciles the tape—maybe tomorrow, maybe a month from now—Carson won't be so very hard to find. He assumes that Super Valu Saver frets about scofflaws who come in the front door, which is a fair assumption from a novice thief.

Super Valu Saver knows better. The major shrinkage happens on the backside, by the hands of its own employees.

Super Valu Saver, Blankenbaker Parkway

A few miles down Interstate 64, Carson finds his next target, a sprawling store fronted by a long greenbelt along the divided parkway. The anger roils in Carson. On the other side of parkway, behind a barrier wall meant to blunt the clamor of traffic, sit the prettiest little houses you ever did see. Behind that wall, the people who live there can pretend that all is well in their bucolic little enclave. Just yards away, Super Valu Saver eats their prosperity.

At the turn-in, a man in weather-frayed gabardine stands on the corner holding a cardboard sign: ANYTHING HELPS. GOD BLESS. Carson loops around the parking lot entryway and comes back to him.

"Hey," he says. "Come here."

Hector sits up, grumbling.

"That dog bite?"

"No, he's a civilized dog."

The man shambles over. His beaten brown lace-ups, several sizes too big, clippity-clop on the asphalt. "What you want?"

Carson nods at the TV in the backseat. *Jesus*, he thinks, *this guy's ripe*.

"You want that television? It's a flat screen."

The homeless guy's face looks like a grimy fist. "Man, what I want a TV for? You think I'm gonna go home and put it in my guest room?"

Hector's ears perk.

"Oh," Carson says, "so it's 'Everything helps except a TV set, God bless,' huh? You can sell the damn thing."

"Naw, naw, man, I got to travel light. What else you got?"

"This isn't a smorgasbord, dude. You don't want the TV, fine. I'll sell it."

"What about the socks?"

"You want the socks?"

"I could use 'em."

"OK, fine. Grab 'em."

The guy walks around the back of the Mustang to Hector's side. He moves his hand toward the backseat, and Hector's neck elongates cartoon-style as he follows the action. The man pulls back. "Your dog ain't gonna bite, now?"

"Mister," Carson says, "he's got better taste than that."

The man grasps the socks. Hector licks his hand, and the man retracts quickly, bag in hand.

"You got any money?" he says.

Carson guns the Mustang. "No."

It takes forty-seven minutes of casing the Super Valu Saver before Carson spots a man wheeling the identical TV model through the parking lot.

"Stay here," he tells Hector, who grumbles in the affirmative.

As Super Valu Saver's exterior cameras roll—one on the facade of the building, pointed directly at them, and two scanning the parking lot—Carson greets the man, who has pushed his wobbly-wheeled cart to the back of a tan Ford pickup.

"Can I ask you how much you paid for that TV?"

"One-forty-seven, I think it was."

Carson looks at the man's hat. RETIRED AND LOVING IT. *Lucky bastard*. "I'll tell you what: I'll sell you that exact same model for seventy-five. I've got it right over here."

The guy studies Carson. "Is it hot?"

"No, I just do my business in parking lots. What do you care? You take that one back, and you've got sixty-two bucks in your pocket."

"All right, let me take a look." They walk down the aisle to the Mustang, and Carson sweeps an arm toward the back seat like a *Price is Right* girl. "See? Same thing."

"All right, then." The retired guy digs in his back pocket for his wallet and counts the bills into Carson's waiting hand. "Twenty, forty, sixty, seventy and five."

Carson lifts the TV from the backseat and deposits it into the cart. "Good doing business with you."

Six days later, the Super Valu Saver security division pieces it together from the videotape:

10:14:07 a.m.: Principal No. 1 (later identified as Carson McCullough) gets into his 2012 Ford Mustang and drives north-northeast until out of camera range. Principal No. 2 (self-identified as Bailey Pruitt) loads the TV into the back of his Ford F-150 pickup and climbs into the cab. The pickup remains stationary.

10:15:02 a.m.: Carson's Ford Mustang enters the image captured by the fixed camera on the back side of the Super Valu Saver store. He leaves the car and tries to open the back door to the storeroom. It is locked. He returns to the Mustang and is seen admonishing a dog.

10:15:47 a.m.: Pruitt exits the Ford F-150, removes the TV box from the back of the pickup, and walks toward the front entrance of Super Valu Saver with it under his right arm. At 10:16:23, he leaves the viewfinder but is picked up seven seconds later by three cameras inside the store. He turns left at the cart corral and queues up at the customer help desk. He is eighth in line.

10:17:01 a.m.: Carson is picked up by an exterior camera as he enters through the front door of the store. For seven seconds, he is out of range, until he emerges into the store proper. Cameras in household goods, bath and shower, women's shoes and electronics track his move from the front of the store to the back. At 10:19:20, he looks left and right and then passes through the swinging doors marked "employees only."

10:21:13 a.m.: Carson exits the back door of the storeroom with a case of Big Chief salmon-and-rice formula wet dog food balanced on his shoulder and propped by his right hand. He places the dog food in the rear seat of the Mustang, stops to rub the yellow Labrador retriever behind the ears, gets into the car, starts it, and leaves. At 10:22:08, the Mustang is out of the range of the camera.

10:24:08 a.m.: Pruitt, now at the head of the customer service line, tells the attending clerk that he bought a TV set from a man in the parking lot and is consumed with guilt about the transaction. He wants to give the TV back. The clerk types on her keyboard. She tells him that she's showing no missing inventory. She speaks into the microphone on her shoulder and asks Billy Cartin, who's working that day in home electronics, to do a manual count of the 22-inch flat screen TVs in his section and then to also count the 22-inchers in the storeroom. He reports back: fifteen. The number matches what she shows in the computer. "Well, sir, it's a mystery," she says. "You can keep the TV."

Pruitt says, "No, no. I'll feel better if I just leave it here." He's out seventy-five dollars, he tells her, but his conscience is clear. She gives him a complimentary coupon for five dollars off his next purchase.

The clerk puts the TV down under the desk, where it's

promptly forgotten until, almost a week later, an assistant manager scans it and says, "Wait a minute. This was in stock at South Hurstbourne. I wonder what it's doing here."

By then, Carson McCullough sits in a jail cell in Daviess County awaiting arraignment, and Bailey Pruitt's legitimately purchased 22-inch flat screen TV has met an untimely demise, fried by a power surge in the home he has shared with Peggy for lo these fifty-one years.

Nothing is built to last anymore.

Super Valu Saver Megacenter, Diann Marie Road

Carson likes nothing about the setup, but having driven the six-and-a-half miles he feels obligated to check it out.

On the backside, the delivery bays sit in a semicircle, half of them actively unloading trucks. Carson sees no way to move inauspiciously here. Further, the sightlines from all directions— the Gene Snyder Freeway, the Hampton Inn behind the store, the access road—are clear. If he's not seen on the premises, he surely will be spotted by someone nearby.

Carson drums his fingers on the steering wheel. "What do you think, boy?" Hector sits diagonally on the passenger seat, his head resting heavy on his front paws. He lifts his eyes to his questioner, his brow arching like a sitcom dad's.

Carson gets out of the car. "Stay," he says, as if Hector hasn't heard that one before.

Inside the store, Carson lingers in the grocery aisles, staring at the beef jerky offerings and yet unaware of his surroundings. What he's been doing this morning feels less like a game and more like something that he ought to find some way of undoing, if only he could. His brain is in backpedal mode. Back to Blankenbaker Parkway, where he lets the old man and his newly purchased TV set go home in peace, where he gives the homeless guy the money in his wallet and tells him to stay strong out there. Back to South Hurstbourne, where the storeroom goes unbreached. Back to Bashford Manor Lane, where he leaves the socks on the shelf. Back to Dan Dempsey—*oh, Christ, Dan, how am I ever going to make this right with you?*—and a spirited endorsement of Timmy Bardo. Back to Cara and profane Delbert McGuinn and Bill Drummond and his own crappy apartment near the Ohio River. Back to his old job. Back to his old life, with its attendant miseries of detached management and lapsed standards and not enough time to get to everything and Jim Jolly's nicotine stink and Molly's incessant absenteeism and the nightly silent terror of wondering if they'll make it, a full newspaper out the door, black ink bled into every open space, the imperfections all too obvious to anyone who cares to look but the triumph achieved just the same. Better to drain out his days there, in the thrall of doing something, than to die out here doing nothing. If he could have it back, he would appreciate it for what it was rather than the mythical what it should be.

Carson shakes his head, clearing the internal monologue. He moves down the aisle to the bottled beverages, and he chooses a small water for Hector and an orange sports drink for himself.

At the checkout stand, he asks the clerk, a pretty girl with pulled-back brown hair and a solar system of freckles on her nose, if she likes working at Super Valu Saver.

"Mostly," she says. "Pay isn't great. But they're helping me go to school."

"Where do you go?"

"U of L."

"What are you studying?"

"Journalism."

Carson considers everything he could say, and indeed, the discouraging words crash into the top of his throat in a jumbled mess. He could tell her about the scrapping and the begging for internships, for jobs after that, for twenty more bucks a week so you're not eating so much macaroni twice a month. He could tell her that the novelty of being the most informed person in almost any room wears out somewhere in your twenties when you realize that your friends have seen promotions, bigger salaries, better houses, good day care for their kids, and that they haven't had to sacrifice nights and weekends to get them. He could tell her that it's all a Ponzi scheme now, that the financials of the deal are so inverted that nobody's going to be left standing. Here he is, proof of that. He could tell her that she'll give up love, ambition, her ideals—those will be swallowed up slowly, but they'll be compromised just the same—for the cocaine high of a newsroom. He could tell her that in the end she won't appreciate the bargain.

He could tell her all of that. And he tells her something else. "Well, good luck with that."

"Thanks. That'll be $2.38, mister. By the way, what happened to your nose?"

He hands her the fiver that Bailey Pruitt gave him.

"Journalism," he says.

Two cameras in the checkout area capture the moment—the conversation for which Amber Trellwin will be complimented in her next performance review ("Engage the customer" is No. 2 in Super Valu Saver's Planks of Success, exceeded only by "Offer the most for the least, every time"), the bemused look on her face as Carson walks away, and his exit.

Four months later, in a plea-agreement hearing, Carson will watch the footage and he will tell the judge that at this very moment, amid all the vexations, he was certain of what he would do next, that the petty crime spree and the self-destruction would end. "I was ready to go home," he'll say. "I was ready to get on with it, whatever it was."

Judge Mason Tingley will take off his glasses and massage the spot on his nose where they grind down the skin, and he will say, "So what happened, Mr. McCullough?" It will be a gentle, searching question, a true desire to understand, perhaps even a hint that ol' Tingley harbors some affection for Carson, who, after all, has endorsed him in the past five election cycles. It's a shame to see things come to this.

Carson will hear the question, will know the answer, but he won't know the words—how to find them, the order to arrange them in, the tone with which to expel them. He'll find no avenue for transferring what lines up perfectly in his head to some system of language that will help the judge see what he sees, to know what he knows. He will simply say, after a few halting starts and a help-me stare at his public defender, "A lot of bad stuff."

Big T—

I don't even know where to begin with this, so I guess I'll just start by not burying the lede: I was a monumental dick to you. Actually, I was a monumental dick to a lot of people, but some of them deserved it. You didn't. That this note is reaching you at the Times proves that you managed to do pretty well despite my distinct lack of helpfulness, but that does not mitigate the main fact, which is, as I've acknowledged, that I was a monumental dick. I'm sorry, man. You deserved way better from me than you received.

I could go into the reasons and the equivocations for why I did what I did, but I'm going to spare you that. I still haven't figured it all out myself, but I'm taking the time to work on it. There's nothing else to do.

Instead, I want to impart a little advice, if you still think I'm the sort of guy who can speak credibly about these things. I would argue that, given all that happened, I'm more credible than ever. But I can't make that determination for you. I'll just throw it out there. Whatever you do with it is up to you.

I'm not blowing sunshine up your skirt when I tell you that you have IT—that elusive concoction of want-to, talent, doggedness and just the right amount of crazy that's always found in the best people in our business. When I hired you, I could see it in your manner and in the way you talked, and I knew we had to have that, if only for a little while. People who have IT don't stay long in a place like ours. I knew you'd burn brightly and then be gone, off to something much bigger. I was right about that, although I couldn't possibly have predicted the way it would happen.

You're also young, T, and that comes with advantages and disadvantages. The advantages are clear: You're in better position to deal with the distinct challenges of being a newspaperman today, when our audience is growing but the dollars our employers make are shrinking. You have energy—metric shit-tons of energy, and I envy you for it. You have that apple-cheeked idealism that I misplaced somewhere along the line and never could find again. Use these things well while they last.

As for the disadvantages, well, they're the same as the advantages. You're going to give your heart to your work, because that's what people with IT do, and then one day it will be twenty years later and you won't be so young or apple-cheeked and you'll have given your heart, and it will be over. You'll be like the former gangster walking to work in his new life, with a wife and 3.4 kids and a picket fence waiting back at home. You'll have happiness and contentedness, possibly the two most debilitating things you can have, and you'll never notice the car rolling up behind you with a shotgun peeking out of the window. I'm speaking figuratively here, of course. In journalism, it's not a shotgun. Just a "new paradigm" or some other such piece of bullshit.

So do the best work you can, T. But don't let them have your heart. It's the best part of you, and they'll never appreciate it.

All the best,
Carson McCullough

Sunday, Late Night

Carson opens his eyes in a mottled-gray world, halfway between sleep and actionable consciousness, the air inside his apartment heavy and dull and choking. He wiggles his fingers, and they feel electric; they tingle and spark and threaten to ignite in the stilled air, and he worries that he's gotten himself mired in a dream. The streetlamps off his balcony dust the darkened room like fine glitter tossed into the air.

When he breathes in, it's at half capacity, and he slides a finger into his left nostril and dislodges the mass of hardened mucus and blood, and air fills his lungs on his next inhale. He uses his thumbnail to flick the booger away.

Carson props himself on his elbows. The room reeks of must and blood and dog farts and the beer-tinged sweat still pouring off him. On the end table sit the culprits, the four bottles of fast-expiring PBR he'd cracked open and poured on an empty stomach as he'd catalogued his troubles.

"You were lucky to be born a dog," he had said to Hector, who sat patiently to receive the bountiful wisdom. "You're born a dog, you remain a dog, you die a dog. That's it. That's your duty. That's your only expectation. Now, don't get me wrong, you're good at it, boy. Nobody's more qualified than you. But I'm just saying that when you're born a dog, you don't have a destiny. You're a dog. You lick your asshole, you eat, maybe you get lucky once in a while—oh, Hector, I'm so sorry I had your balls cut off. Can you forgive me? Buddies for life and all that. I have to tell you, that was a dick move by me. I shouldn't have done it. I should have just allowed you to mount indiscriminately. My bad. Truly."

The drunken-ramble tedium had eventually compromised even Hector's charitable nature, and he had stretched out along the bed while Carson, listing right and slurring words right and left, had hammered one bottle with another in a visual demonstration of the corporate-employee relationship in this lamentable century.

"We define the rules. You do the work." *Clink*. "We decide who stays and goes. You do what you're told." *Clink*. "You thought you had security? Fuck you!" *Clink*. "You thought you could save yourself? Fuck you!" *Clink*. "We will shut you down. Don't like it?" *Crash*. The neck of the bottom bottle sheared off in pieces, large chunks of brown glass that fell to the floor and micro-slivers that settled fine and invisible on the bedspread, on the computer table, into Hector's fur.

"Shit," Carson had said, and he'd collected the larger pieces and disposed of them, then used his hand, unwisely, to sweep the finer leavings off the surfaces of furniture and Hector, who'd already shaken most of them to the ground. As Carson did this, the slivers embedded in the softer places, the webbing between fingers and the flabby sac at the base of his thumb, where the blisters always rose after eighteen holes with his dad. Dots of red formed in these places, and Carson ran to the kitchen sink and its cold-water salve.

As he returned to the larger room, darkness moved in at the edges of his eyes and the room tilted and spun, and he barely made it to the bed before the collapse overtook him.

Jumpin Jacks holds down the corner where Julep Street dumps into downtown proper and widens into a roundabout that takes in the county courthouse and the main police station and the Josiah Rathbone Performance Hall. Tonight, it's a light that guides Carson in with precision (11:18 p.m.) and trivialities (Hostess cupcakes, assorted, 3/$1) writ large in LED, and he picks up the pace—more of a sideways gallop, really, his muscles not quite getting the full signal from his sleep-baked head—so he can return to Hector with some food.

This, he thinks, *is the problem with a late-coming conscience. It's so damned inconvenient.* In Tell City, he'd stopped along the Ohio and heaved the case of dog food into the water, as if to make his transgressions literally sink to the unseen river bottom. The tossed-off act was among a series of devotionals he'd recited on the drive home from Louisville, solemn vows to put the regrettable week behind and start taking things head-on. He'd felt a lifting when the pilfered dog food made contact with the Ohio and burbled down into the muddy drink, a sort of hopefulness he hadn't experienced in a long time, a revival of spirit. That had lasted a few miles. And now, dammit, he needed that food and didn't much appreciate having to hoof it to the corner store to get some.

Inside Jumpin Jacks, in a white-light intensity that renders everything in high-definition clarity, Carson grabs a small can of the beef liver, and he knows Hector's going to raise hell until he can get to the grocery store tomorrow and buy some more of the dog's preferred flavor.

"Anything else?" the clerk asks.

"Two Powerball tickets."

He gathers three packages of the on-special cupcakes. "And these."

"Big jackpot was yesterday. A hunnert and fifty-four million. Do you want to pick the numbers?"

"I don't care."

In the face of indifference, the clerk goes the easy route. The automated sheet comes off the printer, and the clerk hands it to Carson. "Good luck, man. Hey, what happened to your nose?"

"Too much cocaine. Have a good night."

"**B**oss! Yo! Boss!"

Carson squints through the darkness, trying to get a fix on the voice across the street. The figure drops a cigarette, its orange end staring out at Carson as it hits the steps of the Cheerio Lounge. A foot stamps it into nothingness.

"Jolly?"

"The same." Jim Jolly waves him over. "Come have a beer with me."

Carson drops into the street in the wake of a passing car and crosses the divide. The men shake hands like long-separated buddies, with Jolly gripping Carson's shoulder and squeezing.

"You look, well, God, you look terrible." Good ol' Jolly never put it any way but straight up. Carson shakes his head at the memory that tumbles in, of him and Jolly standing on the loading dock after shift one night, Jolly crushing out three cigarettes while they talked about the damnedest thing, how the kid from Wesleyan had shown up for his first shift on the desk, a freshly pressed holder of a B.A. in English, and had never come back from his dinner break. A few hours later, Carson got a one-line email: "It's not for me." And there was Jolly, leaning into the wind, putting it all in proper perspective. "The kid's a piker, Carson," he'd said. "Of course, you're the dumbass who hired him."

Jim Jolly, truth to power.

"Jim," Carson says now. "It's been a week."

"Come on in and tell me about it. I'll buy you a beer. The good stuff. Not that horse piss you drink."

"I can't, man." Carson nods at the sack in his hands. "Gotta get back."

"Come on. A whole bunch of us here. Dobber, Drumley, Boone, Burt."

"No shit?"

"No shit. Just one beer. Those fellas will be happy to see you."

The Cheerio is into irony.

Carson and Jolly step into a darkened dungeon still strangled by tobacco smoke ten years after the city imposed a smoking ban. It's an act that's still a source of great consternation among the citizenry, many of whom grew up on tobacco farms and remain devoted customers of the product. The *Argus-Dispatch* did a great series on the cultural shift when the city fathers decided, in their wisdom, to impose the ban. Carson had been proud of that one, proud of his staff for connecting the Kentucky his father had grown up in with the coming Kentucky—a bit more urbane, a lot more fitness-conscious, and, at least in this city, utterly unwilling to breathe toxins emitted by barstool neighbors.

The Cheerio is a little bandbox of a place, a long bar fronted by stools, washrooms in the back, single black-felt pool table in the middle. Carson is reminded of the George-Bailey-less Bedford Falls and the eponymous Nick's, where they serve hard drinks to men who want to get drunk fast. From the looks of his friends festooned on the far end of the bar, he's way behind.

Behrens spots him first, and the response is as Carson might have expected. He pokes Dobber in the ribs and points at

Carson and Jolly advancing on them. That catches the attention of Drumley and Tomison, and the three of them, with Behrens hanging back, file to the middle of the floor to greet Carson with backslaps and neck hugs and alcohol-imbued breath. Carson, having spent almost a week running away from the corpse of the *Argus-Dispatch*, can't and wouldn't want to hide his happiness at being back among them.

"You girls want to move it along to the bar? I'm trying to shoot here." The guy with the cue stick waggles it menacingly, and the flock of expatriated journalists moves back to the bar, squawking apologies.

"Angry young guy, ain't he?" Drumley sidemouths when they're safely out of earshot.

"Guy like that oughtta be at Skinny's, not here with us oldies," Dobber says.

"Old, my ass," Tomison says. "I could take that guy." The old cops reporter puts up fists, his hands liver-spotted and brittle, and the rest of them shout him down in a chorale of "yeah, yeah" and slaps on his hamster-cage back.

"Hey, boss, what happened to your nose?" Carson doesn't hear the question. He keeps pulling furtive glances at the pool player, certain he's seen the guy before and just as certain that he knows not where. It gives him no solace to realize that the guy definitely knows him, a fact made clear by the well-practiced staredown he employs between shots. Carson takes to ducking his head back into the conversation flowing around him, turning around only when he senses that the guy's back is to him.

Dobber tries again. "I said, what happened to your nose?" Carson looks up, and his erstwhile crew is waiting for an answer.

"You guys really want to know?"

Affirmation comes from grunts, and from Behrens' declaration that he'll listen if it means Tomison will shut up.

"OK," he says, "it was the damnedest thing. It happened

in Louisville." The city name comes out in proper Kentucky dialect, "Luhvuhl," as if Carson has said it with a sheet of paper balled up in his mouth. "I got jumped in the parking lot of my hotel. Two guys. The first one cracked me good in the snout. I was able to fight the other one off, and they both ran."

He shows them the cuticles on his right hand, the outer layer of flesh torn away, patches of angry red in its place. He tells them he did that punching one of his assailants in the damned head, the truth being considerably more mundane. He'd chomped them down to the nub on the nervous drive back home just a few hours ago.

"What were you doing there?" Jolly asks.

"Just getting away, seeing some friends. You guys know how it is. Instant, unplanned vacation." The mumbling acknowledgments come again. "You guys remember Cara Echols?"

"No." The flat denial is understandable from Drumley, who rarely dealt with her. Jolly and Behrens, regular night-shift denizens, nod in remembrance.

"I went up to Cincy and saw her. She's looking good, doing well." Carson's heart drops away at this, at the inadequacy of his description. Why can't he tell them that she looks as if she's slipped into the years like a Saturday T-shirt, that he could feel his heart springing leaks the moment he saw her? For starters, it's unfair that she should be so breezily unaffected by the passage of time, that he should pine for her after one damned email, that she should not feel anything at all for him. To say those things to these guys would be to lay himself bare in a way he never could. But he knows. Whatever's going on with Cara, it's beyond good and well. She's fourteen years gone from here, and it's as if the planet they once occupied together is now his alone. That's how vast her horizons seemed to him, and how small his measured up in comparison.

"You guys getting back together?" Jolly asks. It's a wicked

strike of a question. Carson had never told anyone at the *Argus-Dispatch* about the thing with Cara, and he was sure she hadn't said anything, either. That had been their compact, the agreement that had given them cover to pursue something together. They'd talked about it that first night before he had taken her down on the riverbank, after everybody else had peeled off for home, and they'd negotiated the ground rules. This—whatever they wanted to call the lunches in quiet pockets of Daviess County and the brushing touches that happened beneath the workstation and, especially, below the water surface that long-ago July—was to remain theirs alone. Neither needed convincing that bringing it into the workplace would cede ownership to everybody else, and everybody else's definition of what they were, collectively and independently. It's why Carson had to swallow his pain when she said she was leaving, had to take it and then go back into the office and do his work as if his heart hadn't just been shredded. Why he had to stand alone at her going-away party at Skinny's and shake hands with her like he would with anybody else leaving for some greener grass. And why, when he arrived at her apartment the next morning at six to say goodbye, as she asked him that night to do, she was already gone.

Carson wants to lie and deny it, a spit-take-style "what the hell are you talking about, Jim?" but he can't bring himself to it. The lies have grown old already.

"No," he says, "we're not."

The night grinds on into early morning, and Carson sticks to the diet cola that has made him a joke to the bartender, certainly, and to his buddies as well as they slide deeper into inebriation. *It's worth the grief*, he figures. His head still hasn't cleared from the beers he poured on his barren stomach. *Haven't done anything about that, either*, he thinks, *nor for Hector, who's liable to be pissed*. The played-out air in the Cheerio provides just the barest of sustenance. He's going to have to go, and he keeps inventing reasons to stay.

"You guys find any work?"

It's all "shit no" and "don't want any" and "haven't looked," but soon enough, the deeper answers come. Drumley, as Carson expected, is ramping up a commercial photography business. Tomison, whose final decade at the *Argus-Dispatch* was marked by a desire not so much to keep working but to keep from having to go home to Marnie, is being maneuvered hard by his bride in the direction of an RV and a life of eternal travel (and eternal Marnie). Dobber is up for a job in the county's code enforcement division, a place where he'll do fine, knowing more about the city's laws than anybody currently in the office. Jolly says he's trying to line up some freelance book editing.

Carson looks to Boone Behrens.

"I'm interviewing for the sports editor job in Hopkinsville," he says.

"Isn't that where you worked right out of school?" Tomison says.

Behrens, eyes downcast, confirms it with a nod.

"That's cool," Jolly says. "Complete the circle."

Each guy wears his bravest smile for Boone, but they all know it's about as far from cool as it can be, that a man at his time of life has to go asking at a place he's already been, at a job some twenty-something should have as he starts climbing the ladder. That's what the deal used to be in this business. Carson would hear from time to time about the fortunate ones, like Dempsey, who started at a big paper and stayed there, slowly coming up the ranks. But most of them were like Behrens. They put in their time in the backwaters and the sweatshops, learned how to write a little and sketch out a page, how to beat a deadline, and they knew they'd eventually get called up to somewhere better. The *Argus-Dispatch* was one of those somewhere betters, a place smaller than the *Louisville Times*, to be sure, but where a guy could make enough scratch to buy a house and raise a family. And if there were something more he wanted, he could follow the ladder. But now the ladder's gone, the whole idea of linear progression in their business is gone. The *Argus-Dispatch* is gone.

"I wish it could have ended differently than it did," Carson says.

"We all do, boss." Jolly drains his bottle and signals the bartender for another one. "But, you know, we were in a death spiral for a while. Eight, nine years at least. Probably clear back to when Benny sold us."

Carson shakes his head. "Benny's a money man. I'm not quibbling with that. I'm talking about the work. We still did good stuff, even when things got really lean."

"Lady that lives next door to me sure misses us," Drumley tosses in. "She's eighty-seven, read us front to back every day, says she's just wasting away in front of the TV now."

"Eighty-seven," Jolly says. "There's our target audience. Pretty small. And past the expiration date."

"The hell with that," Carson says. "If we'd been unshackled just a little bit, we could have been more vital than that. Dobber, you know. You think anyone else but us would have filed FOIAs on the school finance stuff, would have been able to figure out how Steener was milking that teat? Shit, man, I had to practically threaten the suits in Paducah to free up the lawyer time for that one. Think what we could have done if somebody who gave a shit ran the place."

"Ah, but there's the problem." Dobber's floppy-eyed and more than a little drunk, and he sloshes his latest Jack and Coke in Carson's direction. "We're the ones who give a shit. Somebody else has the money to actually run a newspaper."

Carson wonders, just for a moment, if he should get into it, if his general policy of what's said in the walls of his office extends this far out, if he shouldn't just bag that final-day conversation with Haller as the spoils of being nominally in charge. And then his untethered tongue makes the decision for him. "Benny told me I could have bought the *Argus-Dispatch* with what was in my 401(k)."

The jaws drop, all of them, right in a line, like something out of a Stooges two-reeler.

"What did you say?" Jolly, having shucked off the role of witty naysayer, looks at Carson with eyes bright and intent.

"I told him he seriously overestimated my 401(k)." Carson laughs, or tries to. It comes out tentative, gaspy. He should have kept his hole closed. These men, only a moment ago all too happy to marinate their discontent in alcohol, now look gaunt and drawn, hungry and desperate, and he's just unwittingly suggested that an opportunity passed right under their eyes. Carson has seen the look before—from Dobber when he got beat on a story by some schmuck in Evansville, from Jolly when Reardon retired and the top job went to Carson, not him. Jolly got over that, eventually acknowledging over a half-dozen beers that it had been the right choice. Carson thinks they'll have to get over this, too.

"But what about all our 401(k)s?" Behrens says. "What if we went in together?"

"Benny has plans," Carson says. "Big plans. Plus, he's already sunk, what, a couple of mil into it, that on top of whatever he paid for it? And shit, maybe he was just yanking my chain."

"Will you talk to him?" Dobber asks. *Jesus, Dobber, too?*

"Tony down at First Commercial, he's my sister's boy," Tomison says. "I bet he could hook us up with some financing."

Carson looks to Jolly, the reliably sensible member of the bunch, for a discouraging word, some context, anything. This thing they're talking about, it's crazy. Nobody starts a newspaper. Not now. The stories of sputtering, coughing, dying papers are legion, the conventional wisdom across all segments of publishing that paper is burning out fast. Carson could sooner breathe rosy cheeks into a corpse than start a newspaper.

"I don't think it can be done," Jolly says at last. "I don't think Benny will let go of it now. I certainly don't think any of us have the first clue how to handle the business end of it. I think we're in the second stage of grief here, and we're kidding ourselves if we think we've still got the fuse to do what we might could have done in our twenties—"

"This is what I'm saying, mostly," Carson says.

"But I also think this," Jolly says, and he looks at Carson, a crooked grin hanging off his cheeks. "I think you might as well give it a goddamn whirl and talk to the man. Because what the hell else is there to do? Boone here doesn't want to go back to Hopkinsville, and from the looks of things, you ain't movin' in with your lady friend."

Carson leaves, a wave at the door and a promise that he'll take this crazy-ass idea to Haller. *What the hell? Gotta talk to the man anyway about this other thing I don't want to do. Oh, and by the way, Jim Jolly can shove a crawdad up his ass for that crack about Cara.*

The side streets are quiet now, brooding and glass-sparkled under lampposts. Carson counts the lights ahead of him, three of them, fluorescent beacons drawing him home to a spartan apartment and what will surely be a livid dog. Carson reaches into his bag and removes a cupcake container, lifting it to his teeth and chewing open a corner. In the rustle of plastic, he doesn't hear the encroaching footsteps.

A chopping blow to the liver drops him, breathless, to the pavement. Carson falls forward, crushing his pastries beneath his girth. The pain, immense and unyielding, blots out the sound. He rolls on his back, arching it as the agony spreads inward, and when he opens his eyes he finds the pool player from the Cheerio standing over him, and utter clarity follows: It's Bradley from the Ford dealership.

"What the—"

Bradley rears back and kicks Carson in the side. It's pervasive pain in triplicate now. "You're a real smart guy," Bradley says. He pulls back for another shot, and Carson rolls toward the approaching foot, trying to take it in the gut. The force knocks half-chewed cupcake from his mouth.

"I know where you live, asshole," Bradley says. Another kick. "I know where you fucking live."

Carson holds his hands out, pleading. "Just—"

"Bet you thought it was cute, filling out that survey, giving me zeroes across the board." Bradley kicks again, and Carson, covering up, takes the brunt of it on the bony parts of his hands. "That's my job, asshole. Probation. No bonus." Another kick lands square in the gut, and Carson's breath is gone again.

"I know guys like you. No honor. No character." Bradley rears back to kick again and then comes up short. He reaches down for Carson's bag, rifling through it and taking the cupcakes and the lottery ticket. "You're done." He spits at Carson, hitting him dead on the mouth. "You're lucky I didn't kill you."

Carson, at last, finds his voice and begins to scream, and Bradley moves up the sidewalk a piece and into the alley, and that's it. Even if the cops showed up now, right this second, Bradley's gone. But nobody's coming. Nobody sees. Night drops in again. The pain sears Carson's innards.

Carson lies back on the pavement, cupping his forehead in his hands, and the booted ribs scream at the imposition. Sweat beads on his face and forehead and rolls toward his eyes, salty and stinging.

The pain from the other shots ebbs ever so slowly, a tide

moving out to sea. But, oh, the ribs. Every breath, and they're coming fast, is a reminder.

And there's this, as the haze clears: *The cops? Yeah, that's not going to happen. Can't happen.*

Monday, Early Morning

Carson's grunts pierce the silence of night as he bucks himself up the stairs. He hangs his right arm loose at his side, trying not to aggravate the rib he suspects is broken, and he grips the railing hard with his left hand, white-knuckled, pulling himself forward and up a stair at a time. Each movement brings another volley of pain, and Carson rests upon each landing, helplessly panting even though that only makes things worse.

Scratching comes from door at the top of the stairs. *Hector.*

"I'll be right there, boy." The words come out raspy and dented by Carson's compromised airflow. Hector scratches with greater insistence.

"Just a sec." Carson holds his breath and jacks himself up the final two stairs to the top of the landing. He exhales in a single blast through pursed lips. He mops his forehead with the back of his left hand and waits for equilibrium.

The keys sit in Carson's right pocket. He tries first to reach around himself with his left hand, but it's no good. The torquing sends the pain into vast new horizons. Next, he dangles his right hand atop the pocket, using his fingers to wrench the flap open. He dips inside, each tiny movement an orchestra of agony. At last, his middle finger finds the key ring. He hooks it delicately and pulls it out of the pocket. Perspiration rolls off his brow and into his eyes.

The transfer of keys from the right hand to the left seems eternal, and it's accompanied by sheer terror about what happens if he drops them. *Slump against the door, tell Hector to save himself and die*, he guesses. Once a clean exchange is made, there remains the matter of achieving some on-the-fly proficiency with using his left hand to perform tasks that have been the sole province of his right. Twice, he bobbles the keys as he tries to fit one in the lock, and twice he racks himself with pain with a herky-jerky midair catch. This is junior high basketball all over again, his doom in his favorite sport spelled out by his utter inability to use his off-hand. "He's going right!" opposing coaches would call out, every single one of them, and damned if Carson wouldn't dribble right into the teeth of the defense.

Still Hector claws at the door.

"Goddammit, boy, give me a minute here." Hector, a tenderhearted dog, whimpers and moves back from the door, nails clattering on the lineoleum.

The door opens, and Carson jams his foot inside it, kicking out. Hector paces along the back wall, ears flattened, mouth caught between a snarl and a cry. As with any dog, Hector's concept of time lacks precision—in the abstract, he would greet Carson in the same way after an absence of twenty minutes or twenty days—but even he knows that nothing about this makes much sense. His man is late, he's agitated, and he's hurting, and Hector keeps a distance until he gets a more reliable signal about things.

Carson heads left toward the bathroom, dragging his arm. He

rifles through the medicine cabinet and the stack of three vanity drawers, until he digs the bottle out from under a towel. The directions call for four ibuprofen tablets, and Carson takes the safety cap into his teeth and tears it loose. He sets the bottle on the counter and digs with a grubby finger until he's pulled five capsules onto the tile. He collects them left-handed and throws the pills back, taking them down his gullet without water.

Hector, watching from the hallway, regards all this, and then he whimpers.

"I know. I'm coming." Carson takes the edge off his voice, or tries to. He's worried for himself, but he's also worried about his dog. *Damn, if I just hadn't seen Jolly on the street, or had just kept going when I did. Hadn't I told Hector he'd be gone just a few minutes? Three hours, it turned out. Hector has a right to be upset, and I have no right to be short with him. This isn't Hector's fault.*

"OK, come on, let's go eat." Every word tears at Carson's side. He eases down the hallway, and Hector flexes his legs, considering a jump at Carson.

"Don't even think about it. We'll both end up lame."

In the kitchen, the pulltop can opens easily enough, and Carson scoops the food out in fingerfuls, dropping it from a three-foot height into Hector's bowl. The dog looks up at him, ears flattened.

"I know."

Hector nudges his free hand.

"I can't bend down, boy. We gotta do it this way."

Carson fills the water dish by pulling the faucet's spray extension as far as it will go and shooting water across the kitchen. As much finds the floor as hits the dish, and Hector goosesteps back.

"Don't be such a baby."

Ears perk.

"It's just water, for Chrissakes."

A cocked head, a quizzical look.

"You lick your own cock. Don't tell me you've got standards."

Hector, a dog who can be reasoned with, accepts this line of argument. He steps lightly back to the food and water and resumes his meal.

Carson, at last feeling numb from the medication, moves, wobbly-legged, toward the bed. He sits down, launching one last searing rush that rides out to every nerve ending. He jostles for a sitting angle that will put the least stress on his ribs. And he watches his boy, takes in the spoiled-meat smell of the liver, and he smiles, a small comfort that squirms into all the bullshit. He has this, his home and his dog, and he thinks maybe that's going to be enough. He has to settle a couple of things, with Benny Haller and maybe with Bradley Bitchcakes, but then it's back to this. After all this time, after all this nonsense, he might not have much to show, but he still has love.

From the kitchen counter, the blinking red LED light on the answering machine beckons with rhythmic insistency. Carson pushes to his feet, the pain nearly leveling him. He shuffles forward.

The indicator shows thirteen calls. Carson presses the button. The messages tumble out. They're tentative, falsely bold, gentle, inquiring. *How are you? What happened? Do you need anything? I can't believe it.* Most of them get erased before the first sentence is unfurled. Then, number thirteen...

"Carson."

Cara.

"Listen, I...oh, God, Carson. Look, I'm just going to send you an email. I have to go. Say hi to Hector for me. I have to go. OK, bye. Check your email. OK. Bye, Carson."

Carson backtracks to the desk. The computer, a no-name PC

with a mortar shell of a monitor that he grabbed in an *Argus-Dispatch* inventory sale, is slow to rouse from its days-long hiatus, and Carson slaps the plastic casing of the hard drive.

The screen flickers. The icons come up one at a time, as if waking eyes. He clicks at the mail logo, and the cursor morphs into a swirl. Carson slaps the computer again. "Bastard!" Hector arches his back and hides his tail under his belly.

The mail folder comes up and populates. The *Argus-Dispatch* will be refunding $15.13 in unused subscription payments— Carson was just foolish enough to believe that if he bought home delivery of the newspaper, even though he carried one home under his arm every night for free, he might somehow keep the enterprise alive with good intentions and happy horseshit.

Next in the queue is Cara's note, optimized for heartbreaking.

> Carson,
>
> I've spent the hours since you left wondering what I might have said to you if you'd stayed a little bit longer. I'm so mad at you right now. I should be preparing for Zurich; I have an important paper to deliver there. But you asked me a question, and I evaded it, and that wasn't fair.
>
> Carson, yes, I loved you. I knew you were waiting for me to say it first. I knew you wanted to. I wanted to. And then my grad school application was accepted and everything changed, and it would have been irresponsible to say it.
>
> But, yes, God, yes, I did.
>
> But here's the thing about that. Your life is there. You knew what you were going to be doing for the rest of your career. You knew Wesley was going to retire, and you were going to take over. Everybody knew it. I remember Jim Jolly telling me one time, "The kid's

gonna run this place." So what was I supposed to do? Ask you to leave that and come with me? Stay?

I couldn't do the first, knowing how much it meant to you. And I absolutely couldn't do the second. I didn't love the job the way you did. I wanted something else. I could have stayed and loved you, Carson, but I would have never forgiven myself if I had. Worse than that, I would have never forgiven you for holding me there, even if the decision had been mine.

We had different places to be. That's all. And it's not fair of you to come here and try to move me back into that place after all these years. It's not right that you're dominating my thoughts now. You did this to me, and now you can't undo it.

I hate to see you unhappy. I hope you'll let me be your friend again.

It was good to see you. It was awful, too. I hope you can understand the conflict there.

Take care of yourself.

Love,

Cara

Nov. 3, 2012

Dear Uncle Peter and Aunt Ruby:

Let me first tell you that I'm doing fine. I know how much you've worried, and I appreciate the concern, but believe me when I say that I'm OK. In some ways, I'm exactly where I need to be.

By now, we've all had plenty of time to reconstruct those last couple of days, and for my part—the only part I can speak to—I'm ashamed that I could not open up and let you know what was going on. I'm ashamed that we fought again over old wounds. When I've thought about the many junctures where I could have changed the trajectory of things, that afternoon in the basement stands out. I'm sorry I followed the same old path.

You know what I've been thinking about a lot lately, Uncle Peter? I've been thinking about things we had in common, rather than the differences that always seemed more pressing. I'm not just talking about Dad. Your ham radio and the scanner stuff. You know, at the paper, we called people like you "scanner rats"—it was kind of a derisive term, for all the people who would call the newsroom to report a house fire or something, when we had the very same information right in front of us. They mostly struck me as police wannabes. But I know that's not you. More than that, though, I guess I'm just frustrated with myself that I never recognized that you and I did the same thing—we listened to the scanner traffic. For you, it was a hobby. For me, it was a professional obligation. But, man, I think we could have talked about that. And if we'd talked about that, maybe we could have talked about other things.

I have a lot of time to think about these things. Mostly, that's a good situation. Some of it haunts me.

Looking forward to seeing you in a few weeks.

Love,
Carson

Monday, Morning

It's early summer on the river, and the town smells of barbecue and brew. Facepainted children dart behind their stroller-pushing mothers, wafts of pork smoke slide across the boulevard. Sunglasses, shorts, tanned legs, fat girls spilling from tube tops, men wearing Dale Earnhardt hats and wraparound sunglasses, wet air, cotton candy, mimes and fortune tellers, a Matchbox Twenty song floating above it all.

Hector, soft-eared and friendly, licks every hand offered, strides about on feet four sizes too big. Cara hooks her arm in Carson's, and she smiles at him ...

"Carson, wake up." A hand finds his shoulder. "Come on now."

Carson blinks twice, clearing the sleep, and finds the face, angular and whiskered, floating above his.

"Uncle Peter. Hi."

The words hurt. His head feels ready to bust wide open. His neck is stiff.

"I saw the car out front and didn't recognize it. What are you doing here?"

"This is my house."

"Yes, Carson, but what are you doing here?"

Carson tries to push himself off the hardwood, a bad idea in every respect. The pain sends him down, panting, onto his back. He pats his chest, finding the folded printout of Cara's note tucked safely into his breast pocket.

"I'm hurt," he says.

His father's brother stands above him in the empty house that Raymond and Suzanne McCullough lived and died in. He pats Carson's dog on the head. "I can see that. You look awful."

"Well, you look good, Uncle Peter."

"Do you need help?"

"Yeah." Carson holds his hands out and clenches his teeth. Peter laces his fingers through his nephew's.

"Ready?"

Carson nods grimly. Peter, all sinew and leather skin, bends his knees.

"One, two, three, pull." Peter drops his ass toward the floor, and Carson rises through uncharted constellations of pain.

Hector scarfs down a plate full of scrambled eggs presented by Aunt Ruby, who says, "You have a fat dog, Carson."

Carson and Peter sit squared off in the kitchen. Through the window behind his uncle's head, Carson can see the backyard of the house he grew up in, the house he still owns, the one he pays a man he's never met a hundred dollars a month to keep tidied up—lawn mowed and watered, gutters cleared, faucets occasionally turned on. Carson can't recall the last time he was here, nor the last time he wanted to be. A couple of years, maybe. Every once in a while, Ruby gets him on the phone and goes to

Carson swallows it down. "Why? It's not like you've got a job for me." *Damn that sharp tongue.* Peter bites his upper lip, raking the skin with his teeth. The regret is instant for Carson, and yet he knows he won't apologize—he can't apologize. Peter hasn't really done anything to him outside of stoically sliding into the roles his own father should have played, and Carson knows he shouldn't hold that against the man. But logic doesn't have much to do with anything when Carson can sit here, forty-eight years old, and be carried back against his will to his adolescent insurgencies against Peter. Now, as he eats a muffin he has no interest in and Peter regards his coffee, Carson thinks about 1980, his first year of driving. His mom about fainted dead away when he dedicated himself that summer to saving enough money to buy a car and came through with it. He must have mowed every lawn on the west side. No afternoons at the city pool, no makeout sessions with Lorelei Lacy, just pure teenage capitalism. Peter, lips perpetually pursed, went along on car-hunting ventures to provide counsel and common sense, neither of which helped much before or after Carson settled on a '71 Matador for $900 ("Get something sensible," ever-sensible Peter had said) and drove away from the quasi-parental bonds till they snapped. A car, even an unreliable one like the Matador, meant Carson could often be where Peter wasn't.

"We called a few times," Peter says. He looks straight at Carson, and Carson looks straight out the window behind him.

"Didn't hear the phone."

"Left messages."

"Been out of town."

It's an exchange informed by the kind of men they are and differences that a generation and aching misfortune have dropped on their shoulders. Peter pokes at the periphery, looking for a way in that he's yet to find in thirty-four years. Carson parries, covering vulnerabilities, real and perceived.

Ruby pours the coffee, keeping them there in stalemate.

"When'd you get the car?"

"The other day."

"Big purchase."

"Not really."

Carson knows where this is headed. Sure as anything, he knows it. Peter has been on him to sell the place since his mother passed in 1994, and honestly, Carson never expected to hold on to it for eighteen years. Now, on this topic in particular, the two of them have become irresistible force and immovable object—Peter, ever logical, not seeing the point of maintaining an empty house, and Carson, ever iconoclastic, taking perverse pleasure in tweaking this uncle of his, confounding him, contradicting him. The McCullough brothers bought side-by-side lots on what was the western edge of town back in '67. They built their homes together, raised families together, Peter holding forth as the pastor at Immanuel Lutheran, Raymond at the aluminum plant. Parallel lives, right up until Raymond slumped over dead and Peter kept on living. Carson came to terms long ago with his feelings on that matter: He resents the hell out of it. For every bit of surrogate-fatherly advice Peter felt compelled to impart in his own Calvinistic acceptance of his only brother's death, Carson registered rejection. Whenever the subject arises and Peter says "a home ought not sit empty like that," Carson doesn't necessarily disagree. But empty it sits just the same.

"You're gonna need some money, I guess," Peter says. "Maybe time to sell that house."

"I'm good."

"What do you mean?"

"I've got a job."

Ruby throws in. "Oh?"

"Where?" Peter asks.

"Running Benny Haller's museum." Carson stands, doing his best to hide his agony behind a toothy cartoon smile, and he grabs the last bite from his plate. "In fact, I gotta go see him today. So if you'll excuse me, I'll go close up the house and be on my way."

In the basement, where Carson stashed some of his parents' belongings that he couldn't see his way clear to selling after his mom died, he finds what he's looking for in the first box he opens. It's his father's U.S. Army-issued Colt pistol, which belonged to Raymond's father before him, a moonshine-running, squirrel-eating wild man from Breck County who couldn't be tamed by Uncle Sam and yet somehow emerged from a dishonorable discharge with the firearm. How it came to Raymond's and then Carson's possession involves a bit of McCullough family lore.

The story Angus McCullough told till the day he passed on in late September 2001, his dying wish to re-enlist and go hunt down *Mooslims*, was that he carried the pistol with him everywhere back in those days, the better to persuade anyone who would intercept his hooch to keep moving down the line. Now, Angus's story was that on one fine June day in '42, he came across Tommy Newton's pack of blue tick hounds sniffing around his stills, tipping them over and making a godawful mess. When he went to shoot the sumbitches—and again, this is Angus's version of the events—the gun jammed and the Newton hounds, a disagreeable bunch of curs, turned on Angus and knocked him down and chewed his nuts off. The other theory, the one subscribed to by near everybody in Breck County not a McCullough or married to one, is that in Angus's haste to shoot him some dogs, he instead fired directly into his own nutsack before he had the gun free. The one certainty, whatever story you believe, is that Angus thereafter had no balls, which is why his contribution to the line of red-headed McCullough boys ended at Raymond and Peter, and why such an unreliable weapon no longer had any place on Angus McCullough's waistband. Raymond, as the older boy, got first dibs on the gun, and for whatever it's worth, Carson could attest that it never once misfired or jammed in all the days that he and his daddy went into his grandfather's fields to shoot rodents.

Carson holds the gun in both hands, arms rigid, and looks down the barrel. "Here it is, boy," he calls over to Hector, who noses a stack of books in the corner.

Before Carson left his uncle's house, he talked his Aunt Ruby out of some ibuprofen and chased them down with coffee. The dose seems to be kicking in. The pain in his side has dulled. He's moving around better. He figures he ought to take advantage while he can.

He curses himself while he looks for ammo. His daddy always taught him to keep guns and munitions separate, a lesson he learned well and carried all the way down into the basement in the summer of 1994 after he buried his mother. Now he's at a loss to remember what he did with the bullets he knows are here, somewhere. He's outsmarted himself.

One by one, he empties the boxes and his memories. He lingers over each item. A photo of Raymond and Suzanne in their first year of marriage, his mom cute as anything in a flannel shirt and a pair of shorts, barefooted on the porch of Angus's house and folding herself into her man, who's all scrawny limbs and big teeth under a ballcap. A floral tablecloth that unfolds into a 1973 summer day on the riverbank. His daddy's electric razor, the one item he rescued from the box his mother had prepared for Goodwill a month after Raymond went into the ground. His mom's favorite Saturday night shoes. These, Carson picks up by the straps with his thumb and forefinger and glances the heels against the concrete floor, the Mel McDaniel song she loved flooding his head.

He unpacks jewelry boxes, photo albums—he dares not open these, or he might as well say goodbye to a day that's barely begun—and old letters and cards, including the entire collection of well wishes that came his way after he graduated from high school in 1982. Regret gnaws at him, castigating him for not taking stock of these things before now. The decisions to keep them had all been snap, a quick up or down as he emptied the house. He barely remembers the hasty rationale.

At last the bullets turn up in one of his mother's hat boxes. Carson thinks it just as well that he didn't make it much farther than the door last night, when he sped over here with poor, baffled Hector, driven by fear and anger and a desire to arm himself and, if necessary, deal with Bradley in the most extreme way. He'd lain across the floor to catch his breath, to find the strength to come down and start looking. Sleep had other ideas. After that, Peter further threw him off task.

In morning's light, it doesn't seem so dire. He'll take the gun and the bullets—he's not prepared, at this point, to vouch for anybody's reasonableness but his own. But he also tells himself he'll be back here as soon as he's healed up, to box everything up again. Maybe he'll transfer it all to a storage unit and go next door and shake hands with his taciturn uncle and suggest a detente. That would be the mature thing, would it not? *Maybe Peter's right*, he thinks. *Maybe it's time to let go.*

Monday, Noon

The old state highway unfurls south parallel to the parkway, and Carson chooses the nostalgic path. He follows Julep Street, past Super Valu Saver and its pregnant parking lot, past the Cracker Barrel and the Fazolis, past the mega-cinema that replaced the single-screen theater of his youth, past the shopping mall stretched out like spider, its anchor department stores on either end, to the abrupt southern edge of town, where development gives way to agriculture. Here, the reason for town's singular growth west is made clear. Boxed in by the Ohio River to the north, the Green River floodplain to the south and the varicose-vein thoroughfare patterns to the east, the city flows in one direction, like a fat man's stomach spilling over his belt buckle.

The cash crops here (outside of tobacco, which still goes strong despite every government effort to choke it out) are corn, soybeans and wheat, and like any good Kentuckian, Carson spends an inordinate amount of his time worrying about what's coming from the sky. The fates have been good to this land so far this year, and as he crosses the threshold and leaves town behind, he's greeted by a panoply of verdant fields and black soil.

Hector sits attentive in the passenger seat, jowls rippling, and Carson ignores the discomfort as he reaches for the dog's loose neck skin and kneads it into bliss. "You remember Benny, boy?" Carson rather doubts that he does. By the time Hector came along, an impulse indulged at an adoption fair at the armory, Benny was deep into his duties as a newspaper executive. The friendship struck up years earlier, when Benny was just a college boy looking to live on his *Argus-Dispatch* salary like everybody else, had been boxed up and set aside— out of respect for every other worker at the place who didn't know Benny the way Carson did, and out of deference to the decisions Benny might have to make. Decisions like selling the paper, or buying it again years later and shutting it down.

At once, it strikes Carson that it all went down a week ago: Mantooth Media's internal memo that the *Argus-Dispatch* had been sold to Benny Haller for "strategic" reasons. Carson's stupendously flawed assumption that Benny planned to restore the paper to what it once had been. Haller's reveal.

One week. And now all of this.

The plan had been to drive out to Benny Haller's country house and say "I'm in," the unspoken part being that Haller had left him little choice. He'd go back and tell Dub and Herman, Boone and Burt and Jim that, *hey, it was worth a shot, but Haller just didn't go for it. He really wants to build that museum to his daddy. Oh, and guess what, I'm gonna run the place.*

Even in concept, that scenario pushes Carson across as just about the biggest bastard in the county, so he amends it on the fly. What if he goes up to Haller's place and pitches Dobber's idea first? Maybe among the six of them, plus some others, plus some financing from Tomison's nephew at First Commercial, they can actually swing it. Maybe they can cover Haller's outlay so far. Maybe they can offer him what he wants out of this deal and still get the *Argus-Dispatch* name and equipment. *How about a Burton Haller museum as part of a living newspaper? Wouldn't that work?* Carson imagines making the whole thing interactive, where little kids could write a story, see it put in the editing system, laid out on the page, spit out by the imagesetter and a flysheet run off on the press, one they could hold in their eager little hands as they headed for the parking lot. *Hell, yes, that would work. It would be even better than whatever Benny has in mind.*

"Hector, my man, I think we're on to something." Carson scratches his dog behind the ears, digging deep, and Hector's back foot thumps against the leather seat.

Carson gives the Mustang some gas, and she drops her rear end and goes, the blacktop ribbon leading the way.

The Haller place sits on eighty acres of premium farmland just across the Ohio County line, on a bald knob that offers a three-sixty view. Benny took full advantage of that when he built the place, commissioning panoramic windows on every side. The Mustang enters from the highway along a straight-shot gravel road bordered on each side by a white picket fence, Benny's turned-out thoroughbreds wandering inside without a care in their pretty heads. (Haller, a man who's chased a few Derbies but hasn't yet won, keeps his prize horses on a farm near Lexington.)

Once the car moves beyond the twin willow oaks straddling the lane, the spaces widen out and the house comes into view. It's massive and intimate all at once, an exterior that in many ways bespeaks humble farmhouse while giving cover to a one-percenter's need for the finer things. Carson remembers coming out here with the other top-line executives thirteen years ago, to the meeting where Benny told them he was going to sell.

Such a bizarre scene, it was, with Benny all business at the beginning as he plainly stated his case for dumping the *Argus-Dispatch*, and then he turned into a preening homeowner as he took everybody around to see the home theater, the indoor basketball court, the lap pool, the sauna. They all walked behind him like stunned sheep. Later, when Carson had time to chew on it, he thought it the one instance of Benny's miscalculating his message. Knowing Benny as he did and, what's more, liking him, Carson could forgive the mistake. Benny thought he was among friends, people he loved and who loved him, but he was wrong. They ceased being his friends the moment he decided to go on without them. The unintended message that day was "look at all this cool stuff, and, oh yeah, I'm getting millions more dollars on the backs of y'all."

Carson pulls the Mustang to a stop and sets the brake. "You stay now," he says, and Hector mumbles discontent but settles into the seat.

It's a chore for Carson to push himself out of the cockpit; the ibuprofen tablets don't last long. He's almost on his feet when the front door opens.

"Carson?" Benny, in a golf shirt and shorts, loafers on sockless feet, bounds down the steps to the gate. "What are you doing here?"

Carson waves and grimaces. "Hey, Benny."

Benny is in front of him now, offering a handshake, and Carson puts out his right hand and grinds his teeth. "What's the occasion?" Benny asks.

"Wanted to talk to you."

"You look a little peaked, man. Come on inside."

"Thanks." To Hector: "Stay here now."

The dog grumbles.

"He won't spook my horses, will he?" Benny looks back at the car.

"Been a long time since Hector's chased anything."

Benny claps Carson's back, and the pain blares out. "I see you took my advice and had a little fun with that money."

"Yeah, well, you know."

"Looks like you've had some other adventures, too." Benny looks him over. Carson knows he's a sight.

"I'm OK."

"All right, Carson, step on in." Benny opens the door, and Carson passes into unadulterated opulence, marble floors polished to such finery that he can see himself stretching out clear across the floor. Inside, it's the perfect temperature, everything in its perfect place, and perfectly clean. Just... perfect. It's such an otherworldly kind of magnificence that it overwhelms Carson's line of thinking as he approached the house, that he and Haller weren't so different when you got right down to the facts of the situation. As young men, they'd chased the same women, laughed at the same jokes, bought the same cheap beer from the Short Stop out on 231, talked about the same kind of aspirations. Maybe Benny had done it to fit in with the crowd as he worked his way up at the paper, but it had seemed genuine enough. Carson had figured him for a friend, a kind of little brother he never had. That played itself out in ways trivial and significant. That first summer, they drank a lot of beer and talked about the kind of place the *Argus-Dispatch* would be when they were in charge—the unspoken part being that Benny would be the kingpin and Carson the dutiful lieutenant. They also chased a lot of tail. In Benny's late thirties, long after the newspaper was behind him, he married a Miss Kentucky two years removed from her stint of royalty, and Carson had a story he couldn't tell about lining up the guy's first lay, the roommate of a girl Carson was dating. He slipped Benny a condom, ribbed for her pleasure, and told him to relax. Just as a brother would.

But now...no. Not brothers. Not equals.

"I should kick off my shoes," Carson says.

"Not necessary, Carson." Haller looks down. "Well, maybe."

C arson surprises himself by getting right to it, no small talk, no throat-clearing.

"I keep thinking about you said, about how I could have swung the paper with what I have in my 401(k)—"

"Well, the name. The physical assets," Haller says. "Maybe."

"Anyway, I was talking to some of the guys the other night, and I told them what you said—" Benny's hands, clasped, begin to grind "—and they were wondering, we all were, I guess, whether together we might be able to buy you out."

Benny's face draws up like a cinched backpack. "Look—"

"Wait, wait, just a sec, I haven't got to the best part." Benny unlaces his fingers. Carson keeps going. "I love the idea for the museum, and you've already announced it and everything, so here's what I'm thinking—and this is just seat-of-the-pants stuff, it could be totally different—but what if we made the museum part of the living *Argus-Dispatch*? Instead of telling people about a dead newspaper, we can show them one that's still going strong—"

"Look, Carson, it's not going strong. I told you this a week ago. I sat there in your office, and I told you that if there was any way to keep it alive, I would have. But there's not, and I won't—"

"But maybe now, when people are finding out what they're missing—"

"They don't care. Jesus, man, you think I just kind of decided, by holding my finger up in the air, that this was how it had to be? You're a good newspaperman and a good guy, Carson, but you don't know jack shit about finance. I had that place looked up and down every which way you can imagine, I had analysts poring over readership data and population trends and market penetration and all kinds of shit, and I'm telling you, there's just no way. If I'd have seen even a glimmer of a chance, I'd have probably gone for it, because that place means more to me and my family than just a bunch of equipment and appraised property, OK? I didn't see it. It's not there."

Carson averts his eyes like a scolded child. "I just thought—"

"Yeah, yeah, you just thought. I just thought, too. I'll tell you something. I was going to walk away. When we were at the due-diligence stage and I saw what the future held, the whole thing seemed like a waste of money. I was having lunch with Reginald Mantooth, and I asked him what he was going to do if I didn't buy it. He said he'd shut you down and sell you off piece by piece—that he knew of a paper in Arkansas that would buy the press, that he could wipe down the computer system and sell it off in parts, the phone system could go over to Elizabethtown, that sort of thing. I came home that night, talked to Peg and my sister, and I decided it couldn't end that way. So I called Reginald the next morning and told him we had a deal. At that point, I hadn't even thought of the museum. But it seems a fitting way to end it. Thought you might feel the same way."

Carson looks up again. "I never meant to suggest that I—"

"What?"

"What I mean is—shit, Benny. It's just not right, OK? We should be putting out a newspaper. You should be running it. We shouldn't be having this conversation, OK? I mean, me and the guys, this was our life. This was what we do. Don't jump my shit just because we want to keep it going. Hell, you should want what we want as bad as we want it."

Haller stands up. "Put on your shoes. Walk with me a bit."

"Don't duck this, Benny."

"Put on your damned shoes, Carson. I want to show you something. It won't take long."

They go out back, beyond the massive, manicured gardens that look as if they belong on an English estate, beyond the chipping green (Carson now flushes a memory of twenty-two-year-old Benny Haller, at the miniature golf course in Evansville, proclaiming "this is way better than the real thing"), down the backside of the hill and into the brambles. The walking is difficult, the path muddy and grown over, and Carson struggles for breath. Benny chugs along, a rotund, gluttonous body riding atop tanned and muscular legs, and in his pink golf shirt he looks something like a grapefruit balanced on two pencils.

"OK, Carson, look," he says. "Let's just play hypotheticals here. Say you were able to swing the upfront money. You'll almost certainly max out your credit to do that. So how are you going to pay for that first shipment of newsprint? The salaries that you'll have to pay while waiting for your cashflow to get rolling? I sold all the delivery trucks. You're going to need some of those. You see what I'm saying here?"

Carson saw it a long time back, in every alternate moment as he drove down here, his mind ping-ponging between his healthy skepticism the night before and the mania today as he thought it might have a shot at coming through. He grunts in the affirmative.

"And do you really think you can get bank financing after what I said about the books? Jesus, man, the bank is going to want to know everything I wanted to know. It's going to see what I saw."

"Yeah, I get it." Carson's words are quiet, meek. "Just forget it, OK?"

"Nope. We're not done yet."

The pathway opens into a clearing, and Benny stops and points at an old shack that lists to the right, about to tumble over on itself, lumber beaten gray by the passage of seasons.

"Here's what I wanted to show you," he says. "My daddy was born in there." Quiet creeps into his voice where bombast once held reign. "Nineteen-eighteen, day before Armistice. My granddad was in Vladivostok, so it was just Grandma and my great grandpa and grandma here to greet him." In the silence that follows, Carson can't stop himself from tallying up the math. He thought his own father had gotten a late start—born in 1931, Raymond McCullough was thirty-three when Carson came along—but Burton Haller had that all beat to hell, delaying fatherhood until his fifties (and until his third, much younger, wife).

"When Grandpa Bertram got back, he got lucky with a couple of planting years and built a little stake." Benny is at the door, or what used to be the door, sliding his palm along the inside of the frame, peering inside. "After that, it was just good timing. Bertram had wanted to go off to college and become a newspaperman, but the war changed his plans. When the crash came, he saw his opportunity, and he bought the *Argus*. A couple of years later, he bought out the *Dispatch* and merged them. By the time Daddy came of age, his path was set. So, too, was mine. All of that happened from this little shack right here."

The implication is obvious, so much so that Carson can't shake the one niggling piece he can't fit into the picture, and he is startled when the question tumbles off his tongue. "Why'd you ever sell? That's the part I can't figure. If it meant that much, why'd you ever get out?"

For the first time, Benny turns around. He backs away from the structure, giving it a respectful distance, and he stands next to Carson. "My family's story is about opportunity, about seeing a chance and taking the risk. That's what Bertram did, that's what my daddy did, and that's what I'm doing now. When a guy came to me and offered twenty-seven million dollars—I know you guys in the newsroom thought it was thirty mil, but it wasn't—I knew it would never again be worth that much, and I had other considerations besides my own. Not investors, but family members who have a stake, and who had no interest in running it. Selling was the right thing for them. Plus, I didn't see the line of succession anymore. Bertram had Daddy, and Daddy had me. But that's pretty much where it ended. Nah, selling was going to happen eventually, no matter what. I did it at the right time, and that money went into a lot of other things that brought some prosperity to this place. Telecoms, hospitals—"

"And we were expendable," Carson says.

Benny puts a hand on Carson's shoulder. It's tender and familiar, and Carson wants to throw up.

"I'm trying to tell you something about my family, about why this museum is so important to me. Carson, I offered you a chance to be a part of this, and I meant that, and the offer stands. But I'm going to need you to get past what's done and get on with what's coming. I'm willing to grant you some leeway, because I know this has been rough, but you've gotta get past it for your own sake."

"I'm trying."

Benny squeezes. "Here's the deal: Come and see me at the newspaper office in a week and let me know if you're in or out. Either way, it's good. If you want to walk, I'll shake your hand and thank you for your service. But if you're in, you're in all the way. I want you to put your heart in this thing. You get me?"

Carson forces a glance to his left, so Benny knows he's been heard, and he nods. Benny lightens the grip on his shoulder. "Had lunch?"

Monday, Afternoon

Just down the highway a piece from the Haller place, Carson pulls the Mustang to the shoulder and gives in to what his body has threatened all day. He opens the door and leans out of the bucket seat, as far as he can reach, the cartilage and the bone in his midsection screaming at the demand. His head safely out, his body dangling off the seat belt, Carson yaks it up. All of it. Benny's cold cuts, Aunt Ruby's muffin, the peanuts he'd snorked down in elephantine bliss at the Cheerio, thirty-two flavors of stomach acid, the fear and hate he's been swallowing in perfect little capsules.

"Jesus," he says, his lips thick with the leavings of acidic drool. He tosses his head back and swallows, and a fresh wave surges from deep inside—from the bottom of his feet, it feels like to Carson—and sprays out of him like soda from a shaken bottle.

Hector, a sympathetic dog, whimpers and hides his snout under his front paws.

"I'm good, I'm good."

Carson, head oriented to the ground, reaches over with a

flailing arm and pats his dog on his waiting head. "That's a good boy," he gargles.

The odor that rises up is suffocating and rancid, as if Carson has been carrying it all through a slow degradation inside him. He sets his head back on the seat and thinks he can smell smoke on his skin from every cigarette ever lit at the Cheerio. He closes his eyes and tries to tune in the signals from his body. *Are we done here?* Slowly, slowly, the tension pulls back, his breathing settles, and his agitated mind clears like clouds rolling away in time-lapse photography. All the while, Carson works the skin on Hector's neck, until the dog has slipped the bonds of consciousness.

Carson opens his eyes and looks at himself in the rear-view mirror. It's sixty-some degrees, and his face is wet and gray and bloated, his eyes translucent like blown glass. He reaches for the key and starts the Mustang, and he eases her back onto the road.

The car heads back to the house on Worland Street. This is inexplicable to Carson—truly baffling, even though he's the one who veered west off Julep Street, onto the turnpike, toward the western end of town. His mind shouts him down, tells him to take a side street and work his way back to downtown, to home. His hands and feet ignore the admonitions, and onward he goes, to Saddleback Road and the tracts of houses his father and his friends' fathers built by the score in the 1960s, forming their own enclave of suburban living in a town too small for an actual suburb. For men of certain means, fortunate enough to hold jobs at places like the college and downtown banks and law offices and the aluminum plant, the west end became a respite and a world away, close enough to the town proper that it wasn't a hardship to get there, far enough that each family could have the illusion of its own bluegrass kingdom. Carson lived among these low-slung houses and perfectly trim yards from 1967 to 1982, from three to eighteen. In the successive years, he has come to believe he was the only one who saw the irony that Bluegrass Acres, the oh-so-Kentucky name affixed to his childhood neighborhood, came to be only after the actual bluegrass acres of a working horse farm were paved over with an org chart of nested lanes.

At Gatewood Junior High, Carson's adolescent alma mater, he turns left, followed by an immediate right onto Pennyroyal Avenue and, finally, another left onto Worland. The sightlines have changed from what they project in Carson's memory—for example, the Sumners' house, absent of any Sumner for almost a quarter-century, is blue now rather than brown—but the angles align perfectly with his recollection, his parents' house and Peter's house beckoning at the end of the block. Peter's holds down the corner, Raymond's tucked just inside. Carson sees this and the old black dread returns again. When Raymond was alive, Carson would walk from school along this route, coming home just an hour behind his father, who dragged in after first-shift work at the plant. It was the best part of Carson's day, throwing open the front door and finding his father there in the embrace of a beer. Raymond, bone-tired and beaten down, would throw him the football, or pace him through his spelling words, or chatter ceaselessly about the Wildcats—Carson was a Kyle Macy devotee, while Raymond's allegiances ran a generation back to Cliff Hagan.

And then, on March 24, 1978, a Friday, the world as the McCulloughs knew it tumped over.

Carson's chest tightens around the memory, trying to hold it down—as if he could ever forget, as if it doesn't pierce his thoughts every day that he wakes up and is older and alone. The day had blown in cold, one of those startling, wintry days that uncommonly barrel through the Ohio Valley before the full bloom of spring. Carson had walked home leaning into the wind, more eager than usual to see his pop. The Wildcats were in the next day's Final Four, a fact that had come to dominate life in the McCulloughs' house, and every other house Carson knew of. If the Wildcats could get past Arkansas—Carson remembers the strangling youthful fear that they would not be able to do so, that Joe B. Hall was a too-slight successor to the great Adolph Rupp—then it would be on to Monday and Duke or Notre Dame.

Raymond sliced the previous night's pork shoulder and asked about school. All these years later—thirty-four of them, each more difficult than the last—Carson has the conversation front of mind as if he had taped it, which he did, in a manner of speaking. After Raymond hit the floor, after the ambulance, and his mother's anguish when she came home with the groceries, and Peter and Ruby's holding them deep into the night— after all of that, Carson had written it all down, everything he remembered, and in the ensuing years when he would feel as though bits of it were slipping away from his recollection he would find the notebook and read and memorize the details anew. If God couldn't or wouldn't keep Raymond alive, Carson certainly intended to.

And so the memory goes, again.

"The Tygart boy still giving you trouble?"

"Not so much, no."

"You tell him what I told you?"

"No."

"You tell him. He's a bully, son. And bullies understand nothing like they understand a sock to the nose. Tell him to leave you alone, or else."

"Yeah."

"Scary to think about that, isn't it?"

"Yeah."

They stood in the kitchen, backs to each other, Raymond

slicing the meat, Carson spreading the white bread with mustard and mayonnaise. Carson didn't see the next part, only heard it. A little gasp and Raymond fell forward, dead as dead can be. His nose and mouth crashed against the kitchen counter, and that turned the son around in time to see the father crumple halfway into the lazy susan. It was such a bizarre thing to see, as incongruent as opening the refrigerator and seeing a horse gallop through the potato salad, that Carson thought perhaps Raymond was playing some sort of game. Only when Carson got him out of the lazy susan and saw it all, the bloodied nose and the crashed-out teeth and the eyes dead like the rest of his father, did he scream and then run, adrenaline surging, to get his Uncle Peter.

And now, as Carson pulls into the driveway, he watches the fourteen-year-old version of himself, in a white Wildcats tee with blue trim and brown-and-green plaid pants and stocking feet, a plump boy even then, a scattershot of acne scars across the jaw, run across the front of the garage on his way next door.

Hector settles his chin into his master's thigh. Carson sits with his back against the east wall. The cloud cover has blown away, and light beams through the basement window on the backside of the house, casting half of him, and all of Hector, in hazy white.

A photo album, faded red and frayed at the edges, sits on Carson's other knee, balanced underneath by his right hand as his left turns the pages. The clear plastic covers have gone brittle with age, the photographs they shield now immovable in the glue that has hardened into thin orange rivulets across the cardboard page.

His mother started this when Carson came screaming into their lives, a baby that defied the boundaries of medical science as it had been explained to her and Raymond. Suzanne

McCullough aimed to turn their beautiful, unexpected boy's life into a documentary in still frames, and so the Carson in the pages moves left to right across them like the ascent of man. On his back in a crib festooned with bunnies. Crawling across the shag carpet of the rented house on Chokecherry. Standing wobbly-legged in his grandparents' shack and held up by the phantom hand of Angus McCullough. Legging out a single as a first-grade tee-ball player.

Suzanne is an infrequent subject in the photos. His mother, Carson remembers, was almost always the one behind the camera, making sure she had some proof of their father-son hijinks. When she does show up, it's the three of them together—like this, a photo of the family on the steps of the Ryman Auditorium, Suzanne in a dress made for summertime, aqua-blue scarf in her hair, ever-present sunglasses, her arm across Carson's chest, Raymond's hand on his shoulder and hers, the three of them a unit. *Who took this?* Carson cannot remember, can barely pull the larger details together in his own mind. *Was this the year we went west to Texas or east to North Carolina?* Suzanne would surely have written it down on the back of the print, but seeing that is not a possibility now.

As his mother lay dying, Carson went to her and tried to make amends for having been more his daddy's boy than hers. He felt as though he owed it to her to make some accounting for the time he had denied her, now that the days he always thought would be there were draining out. She would have none of it. "Everybody loved your daddy," she said in gasps and cracked syllables. "Why wouldn't you love him more than anyone?" She was almost dead by then, the moments of lucidity whispers in time, and Carson tries to cherish the words for what they were, another example of Suzanne McCullough's subjugating her own interest for her son's. He was alone with her when she went, and then alone with himself—at thirty, old enough to be left to his own devices in the world but far too young to know what life was going to bring his way.

"You're back."

The voice from the top of the stairs sends a charge through Carson and brings Hector yelping out of sleep. Peter bounds down to the landing. He's spry for his years, the result of good genes, a clean life, and a daily "constitutional," as Peter calls it, a three-mile out-and-back walk to his church downtown, where he's now pastor emeritus. This he does rain, shine, heat, and freeze be damned.

"To what grace do we owe a second visit in a single day?" he asks his nephew, the seeming corniness of the line lost on both of them, for this is how Peter really speaks when a moment of whimsy catches him right.

Without words, only an outstretched palm, Carson invites his uncle to sit. Peter folds himself neatly on the floor.

"Looking through some old photos of Mom and Dad," Carson says. "I don't know. Feeling a little—well, detached, I guess."

Peter leans in, close enough that Carson can smell the dabbed-on aftershave. He taps the page twice, beneath a photograph that lacks definition, a dark, long-distance, out-of-focus shot that mostly takes in the back of a head. "Spelling bee?"

Carson can scarcely believe it. It was just a few minutes earlier, as he really studied the picture, that he saw Mrs. Spurgeon, his sixth-grade teacher, in the front row and pieced together the story of the shot.

"How'd you know?"

"Sixth grade, wasn't it?"

"Yes. Come on. How'd you know?"

"Well, there you are." Peter points at a photo on the opposite page, one of Carson in a blue velour shirt and brown jeans, his legs crossed under him as he sits, leather lace-ups on his feet. "See the flag over you there? Says '76.' Sixth grade, right?"

"Yes. But the spelling bee, how—"

"Let's see if I remember this." Peter strokes his beard. "'Bivouac' to set up the winning word, correct? And that word was 'hyacinth,' right?"

"There's no way you—wait a minute, Uncle Peter. How'd you know that?"

"It was in all the papers." Peter gives his nephew a nudge, enough to send a tinge of pain sliding through his ribs.

"No, seriously."

The mirth leaves his uncle's eyes, the mouth flattens out, and he's back to the sober man Carson has known all his life. "Raymond. Raymond talked about it all that spring, wouldn't shut up about it, if you want to know the truth. 'My boy is the best speller in his school.' If you'd known how hard school was for him, you'd know how proud he was that it came so easily to you."

It's quiet between the two of them, the basement cavernous in the silence, with Hector's swishing tail the only noise until Carson, at last, finds his words. "I didn't know. I mean, I knew they were proud of me, but—well, I just didn't know."

Peter flips the page over, and now Carson is in an oversized white shirt, feathered hair, wearing an affected sneer for the camera's benefit. He remembers this. His first school dance, which he spent along the gymnasium wall with Stevie Woodberry, talking about the Wildcats.

"That's the problem with us McCulloughs sometimes," Peter says. "We think what's clear to us is clear to others, and we don't always say the words someone else needs to hear. Don't be too hard on the memory, Carson. It goes way beyond your dad, and he did better at it than our dad did. He did better at it than me, too."

Carson turns the page. Raymond, mostly gray-haired by now, wraps a meaty arm around his boy's shoulders. Behind them, the stock cars cover the dirt track. Sweat pools in the armpits of Raymond's shirt and on Carson's lip above those big white teeth he shows unabashed.

"I feel like I've forgotten too much, that if I don't force myself to remember him, I'll lose him," Carson says. "Mom, too, but I had longer with her. And then, you know, I'll catch myself in the mirror or something, and there he'll be, looking back at me."

"Your Aunt Ruby said the very same thing this morning. You got his face, that's for sure."

Carson's mind is like a leaf on the breeze, bobbing from present-day mirrors to long-ago classrooms and his own sense of isolation that was partly a product of the age he was when he lost his dad and the peculiar distinction that gave him. That year, 1978, he was the only kid he knew who'd lost his dad. Sure, some kids had no father at all, or shitty fathers they wished they didn't have, or stepfathers who paid them no mind. But he was the only one who had a father one day and not the next, who had to batten down his emotions to the classmates who suddenly gave him a wide berth out of pity. The way Carson figured it, there was no good age to lose a father, but fourteen was certainly among the worst.

"I was angry at God," he tells Peter. "I still am."

"God can take it."

"I hate it when you say that."

"It's simple, but it's true."

"It's bullshit." Carson's voice rises, and Hector decamps for the other side of the room. "It's a pat answer designed to soothe simple minds. 'Oh, OK, God can take it, yippee!' Come on, now, I want you to lay it out there for me. You've been dying to talk to me about this, so let's go. If God really exists, why's he such an asshole? I look around, and I don't see much evidence of this God you believe in, Peter."

"God can take that, too."

Carson pushes himself up and kicks a stack of photo albums.

Yellowed, brittle paper scatters in their wake. "Get off it, man. Bring it to me, convince me. I think you're scared to know the truth. I think it's far easier for you to sit here and say 'God can take it,' to be comforted by this idea that there's a benevolent God who loves you. But you're not willing to get up close and really get to know him, because you'll find out he's not there, and that terrifies you."

Peter's voice drops in register proportional to Carson's increased shrillness. "Why are you so angry?"

"I'm not angry. I'm tired of the lying. You've always wanted to talk about this. Well, come on, then. Let's talk about it: I think your God is an invention to make you feel good, to give you something you can point to when you can't explain it any other way. He's a crutch."

"You really believe that, Carson?"

"Absolutely."

"Let me ask you something, then."

"Shoot."

"You have such certainty. You know everything there is to know about God, which you say is nothing because he doesn't exist. You are completely at ease with everything he is, which is nothing because he doesn't exist. Does that about cover it, Carson?"

"Yeah."

"You're much more certain than I am, then. I have doubts—deep, troubling doubts about God and his plan. You know, what I have to go on is scripture that, frankly, seems more allegorical than factual to some people—me included—and a deep faith that is tested every single day. I sometimes feel as though I don't know him at all and don't understand why he lets horrible things happen. But you—you have certainty. You say I invented God, but I'm not the inventor here. You are. You've invented an absence of God that you can blame for everything that hasn't gone your way. In case you hadn't noticed, Carson, you're not alone in your disappointments."

"Don't patronize me."

"Raymond was my brother. Suzanne was like a sister to me. And you—"

"I'm a disappointment, huh? Surprise of the century."

"—you seem shocked that it's a nasty world out there, like it's singling you out or something. Pardon me for saying so, but that's a sad way to live. You should grow up. It's long past time."

Carson turns from his uncle. He kneels into a squat, and it's shooting pain into his side again. He grinds his teeth. He stacks the albums again, sliding the separated photos between the heavy cardboard pages. Peter watches him. Hector watches him. He snaps his fingers, and Hector wobbles up and comes.

"I'm leaving," he says, head down. "I want you out of my house."

Monday, Late Afternoon

Carson takes the back way home and scolds himself. Past the signposts of his youth—the J.B. Shanks Pizza Palace that became a Jimbo's Shrimp Shack and, finally, the Disco Inferno Vintage Clothes that it is today. Past the grown-over infield mounds that were once the drive-in theater, the big screen long since gone and the speakers sheared off the tops of the poles. Past the armory and Ricketts Park and Catholic High and the tangled back alleys that snake through the gut of town behind the hollowed-out antebellums. Carson talks to himself in a growl, one that disconcerts Hector.

"Stupid, stupid," Carson says, smacking himself in the forehead with the heel of his hand as he idles at a stoplight. In the next lane over, four teenage girls in an Explorer giggle at him, and he gives them the finger.

It shouldn't have gone the way it did. Carson doesn't know much, not anymore, but he knows that. *Jesus Louise-us, I'd gone back to collect some things, to shore up my thoughts, to walk next door and tell Peter, you know, you're right. Maybe it's time.*

But no. Peter intruded again, as he had so often before. That's the history. Carson, searching and wanting and not knowing how to break through the self-imposed obstacles. Peter, overreaching, charging in, dripping self-confident wisdom and sanctimony in equal dollops. They were too deep into the game to change tactics now, either one of them.

The next light brings Julep Street, bending toward the river, toward home. Carson turns up the radio, and Barry Bowersox tumbles into the front seat. The show is winding down, and Carson gives a silent cheer for his good timing.

"You're on with Barry Bowersox."

"Uh, yeah, I'm an *Argus-Dispatch* employee." Carson turns it up. *That's Jim Jolly, sure as anything.*

"*Were*, friend. You *were* an employee. I wish I could say I was sorry for your loss, but I'm not."

Carson steers the car onto Julep Street. Hector yawns.

"Shush, boy." Hector, a dog who knows his liberties, yawns again.

"Well, OK, Barry, there's another cheap shot—"

"The truth is never a cheap shot."

"Are you going to shut up and let me talk?" *Good old Jolly.* The guy was well into his own career when Carson showed up at the paper, tube socks under his chinos and a lip he didn't have to shave more than once a month, and Jim let him know right off that he wasn't near up to snuff for the job. Jolly has never countenanced fools.

"Go ahead."

"OK, look, even if you're right about the bias and the leftist agenda and all that—and you're not, by the way, but let's just pretend that you are. Even if all that is true and the *Argus-Dispatch* offered nothing redeeming to the civic life of this town, don't you think it's just a little unseemly to be on the radio, day after day, and be joyous about all of these people losing their jobs—good jobs—in an economy like this one? I mean, God, I'll probably never work in that field again, and I'm fifty-eight years old, which means I'll probably never have a career kind of job again. And I'm just one guy. There were scores of us. Doesn't that bother you? Don't you think it would be, I don't know, decent to just move on and let these people have some peace?"

Carson rocks in his bucket seat and pounds the steering wheel with his fists. *Yes!* It's only the movement of traffic that keeps him from unbuckling, stepping out into Julep Street in front of God and everybody, and saying "You hear that? Huh? You happy now?" *Damn. Good old Jolly.* The cantankerous old so-and-so, the one guy Carson would have never let go if the *Argus-Dispatch* had lasted long enough, has eroded Bowersox's high ground as a man of the people. *That asshole is rooting for failure, the very sin he accuses the newspaper of committing.*

Bowersox comes back into it. "I'm going to answer your question, friend, and then I'm going to turn it over to the good listeners out there, who just lit this place up like a keno board in Vegas. Now, here's my answer: It doesn't bother me one little bit. This is America, Jack, and you have to be strong to stand here. The people who were really good at their jobs at the *Argus-Dispatch*—and I've never denied that it was once a great newspaper—they left long ago, to their graves or to jobs more fitting their excellence. The ones who remained, and I have to presume that you're one of them, ran this thing into the ditch. So listen to me, pal, and listen to me good: You aren't good enough. You. Your friends who are now out of work. You weren't good enough, and that's that, and it's too bad for you. And aren't you lucky that you live somewhere that the liberals you love have set it up where you can eat at the government trough for the rest of your days? You ask me to let you have peace. I say, friend, that you've got it backward. Why don't you let me have some peace, you unrepentant freeloader? It's not enough that I have to feed my own family. I have to feed you, too? You wonder why I'm angry? There it is. I'm tired of carrying you, and my listeners are tired of carrying you. That's what I say to you, friend."

Bowersox then throws the switch and starts letting the sheep into the barn, one by one by one.

"Barry, I'm with you one hundred percent. These liberals..."

"Barry, way to go! You sure told him..."

"We have to stop them, Barry. If we want to preserve our way of life..."

"Barry Bowersox for president..."

Wave upon wave, the fellationists fall at the altar of Bowersox, currying favor with this patchwork of a man—short-order cook, chemical salesman, manure truck driver, all diverse jobs with a single commonality, and it's that Barry Bowersox was singularly terrible at them. Somehow, this man who fell into radio has grabbed the stage in a paranoid, angry time and become the mind of those who cannot think for themselves.

The supplicants and mendicants call out to Bowersox, and Carson swings the Mustang around for a big, illegal U-turn in Julep Street, angry horns in symphonic harmony calling after him as he drives hard toward the transponder on the horizon.

B arry Bowersox sends out his signal to sycophants from a squat slate-gray brick building on the southern edge of town. Carson sits in the Mustang, tucked into the rows of cars in the radio station lot, and he checks the pistol clip once, twice, three times. Hector noses at the gun—it makes noise, and noise means a game—and Carson shoos him away with a quiet "not for you, boy."

Bowersox comes through the car's speakers in a dialed-down hush. He has moved on from the *Argus-Dispatch* to a medley of right-wing outrages. The erosion of traditional values, the coming police state of the United Nations, the intransigency of this shadow administration, armed illegals taking the streets if we don't do something about it. He ladles it up and pours it into the airwaves, and if your particular brand of paranoia isn't in the offing, just wait. Barry Bowersox will get to you.

It wasn't always this way, Carson thinks. When Bowersox started his first talk show in '98—he was selling ads for the station and persuaded management to give him an eleven p.m. to two a.m. slot that would have been taken up by some syndicated show out of Chicago—he was fresh and interesting and local. The folks who worked while most of the town slept at last had a connection to the place they lived, somebody who understood their lives and struggles. Convenience store clerks, waitresses, third-shift guys at Peabody, cab drivers—hell, newspaper production staffs. All had a friend in Barry Bowersox.

As his popularity grew, the station steadily moved him back on the clock and stripped away his ad-sales duties, until he found the 9 a.m. to 4 p.m. slot and became the station's single biggest source of revenue. In an *Argus-Dispatch* profile, he proclaimed "Not bad for a boy from Calvert City," and no one disagreed. And no one could have imagined the hard rightward shift coming.

When the planes crashed into the towers and the Pentagon and a field in Pennsylvania and a nation went to war, Bowersox felt the pull of a campaign against Islam, the fulcrum of which was his contention that "Muslim men are the pit bulls of society—not all of them are vicious, but for safety's sake you have to assume that they are." Western Kentucky's more liberal element, a measurable if reticent population, came unhinged, with demonstrations at the station and a bumper-sticker campaign that can still be seen on the odd Ford Festiva around town. The *Argus-Dispatch* came out against Bowersox in an editorial, severing what had been a mutually admiring relationship. Bowersox's ratings went up four points, and the radio station doubled down behind him. Several years later, when a black man became president and the nation became a hotbed of constitutional scholars, Bowersox's empire was complete, a frothy mixture of capitalism (*Bowersox T-shirts and weekend survivalist classes, available now online!*), fear-mongering, and an unyielding demonstration of how that no-account guy over there is skating by on your hard work, drinking from the glass you fill, and doesn't that just make you sick? All of it powered by thirty-five-thousand watts.

Carson checks the gun again and shows it to Hector. "What do you think?" Hector sets his chin on his front paws and mumbles.

"It's time for equilibrium," Carson says to no one.

Bowersox is at once instantly recognizable and deceptively insignificant when he emerges from the station. The drawn-back hairline on the slab-of-granite head looks the same as it does on billboards around town, from which the munificent Barry Bowersox smiles down upon his good people. But here, in person, the eyelids sag and crags ramble across the map of his face, undeniable evidence that a touch-up brush can't hide the manifestations of seven hours of daily chatter and the pots of coffee and bags of french fries that push him through his days. As Bowersox lumbers on little-piggy legs toward his Lexus—itself a caricature with its Bowr Powr plates, not to mention easy to find for a man of Carson's intentions—he is moving in slow motion through the white noise clouding his own head. Bowersox is an easy mark, even for someone who approaches him from behind on choppy feet, trying to outrun a steady loss of nerve.

Two things happen when Carson puts his right foot in the small of Bowersox's back. First, the radio host hits the asphalt the way a sack of potatoes might, a lumpy, dumpy *ooomph* of a fall onto his stomach, and Carson has the presence of mind to drop on top of him and sink a knee into Bowersox's neck to keep him from turning his head. Second, Hector, an observant dog, sees the collision and goes fuck-all nuts with the barking.

"*Shut up!*" Carson turns his head and sprays the words at the dog. Bowersox wriggles beneath him and lets go a muffled scream, no match for the seventy pounds, easy, that Carson has on him. Carson sets the barrel of the gun against the back of his head. "Shut up."

Hector's yelps still come like a skipping record. *Barkbark barkbark barkbark.*

"What do you want?" Bowersox asks. His words shimmy and threaten to diffuse as they emerge. "I have money."

"I know you do." Carson chambers a round, and Bowersox breaks into a thousand pieces, his crying and begging making a nearly unintelligible mess of his words.

"Pleasedon'tIhaveadaughterpleaseohpleasedon't—"

Barkbark barkbark barkbark. Carson knows he's running out of time.

"Do you think I give a fuck about your daughter?" Carson's own voice comes in a haggard rattle as rage and fear flood his senses.

"No. Please."

"What was it you said? Oh, right: 'It's not enough that I have to feed my family. I have to feed you, too?' " Bowersox has no dignity left. He brays like a coyote, a long, sad, lonesome wail that's reaching no one.

"You need to learn not to kick people when they're down, Bowersox. In the next life, maybe you will." Carson pushes the snout of the gun into the soft flesh where the back of the neck meets the skull. Bowersox tries one last time to throw him off.

"Goodbye, Barry." Carson pulls the trigger, and the mechanism of the Colt works perfectly. The hammer strikes the firing pin, which moves forward in the chamber to where the bullet would be had Carson not emptied the clip. The barrel bushing pushes out, knocking Bowersox's head forward and mashing his mouth into the ground. The magazine attempts a reload with bullets that aren't there. Bowersox has half a second in which to realize he's still among the living, and in that time, he dumps his bladder into his pants and down his leg, where the urine drips out next to his shoe before Carson brings the Colt's handle down on the back of his head. The stars come out in Kentucky, Bowersox lies stilled in his own water waste, and Carson is on the run back to the car as Hector barks and barks and barks.

Monday, Evening

Carson has chosen a beautiful night to throw his life away. He sits beside the Ohio River, legs drawn up, left arm across the back of Hector, who leans into him. The water burbles westward, a rippling black sheet, under a black sky holding the new moon. Up and down the river, here and on the Indiana side, he sees spectral, gauzy lights of distant houses and storefronts. To his left, the west, his city burns, casting a white glow over the treetops. He is surrounded, and he is alone.

The kinesis unspooled by the Bowersox beatdown followed Carson's expectations. He was in his apartment, packing up a few days' worth of clothes for his escape to wherever, when Bowersox broke back onto the air to report his own assault and battery.

"I didn't see him. He had a dog. He worked for the *Argus-Dispatch*, I'm sure of it. His gun jammed or I'd be dead."

To the extent that Carson had planned this thing at all—not very damn much—he had counted on Barry Bowersox to be prideful. His taking to the airwaves and spilling details the cops would just as soon hold close would give Carson time to slip out of town as the police worked backward, coaxing Bowersox out of the studio and questioning him at length before beginning the process of deduction that will, inevitably, lead to one particular man and one particular dog. Carson has no illusions about that. He's going to jail. He simply wants a few more hours here, alone with Hector, in the little cove where a younger man and a younger pup and the woman they both loved would while away summer days that seemed as though they would stretch on forever.

Every now and again, a car blows past on the highway above, and Carson holds Hector a bit tighter. Terror lurks in everything now—the fear of being seen, identified, pointed out, cast away—and Carson realizes that this is his new reality. He wishes he could remember what it was before this.

Hector sinks into the mud and rests his chin on Carson's thigh. Carson threads fingers through the tufts of hair on the dog's head and slides them against the bias. More than anything, he worries for Hector. *Who will take care of him?* Peter probably would, grudgingly, if asked. *Cara? Benny Haller?* Carson conjures an absurdist vision: police on a bullhorn urging him to come out of the cove with his hands in plain sight. Carson, desperate and hungry and badly in need of a shower, intent on negotiation. "I want three things: a ham sandwich, a job on the prison newspaper, and a loving home for my dog!"

Carson puts his head on his knees and he weeps.

Where does a man first go wrong? The urge to sleep hangs heavy on Carson, and he fights it off by looking for what connects the man he was with the man he is now, a bone-cold fugitive on a windy night on the river. The simple answer, of course, is that he set this course when he lifted that first paperback at Super Valu Saver, a juvenile exercise in petty revenge and thrill-seeking. But Carson finds no solace in simple answers. He's forcing the aperture wider.

Did he cast his lot when he took that first (and last) newspaper job, with the stated desire to keep himself steeped in compact discs and discount pizza for the remainder of his days? Even then, twenty-six years ago, many of his classmates—even the spectacularly dumb ones—saw more of the horizon than he did. He ran hard toward immaturity, an unwillingness to even try to stretch himself once career inertia set in, and he stayed there. Every time he didn't leave the *Argus-Dispatch* when he had the chance pushed him deeper into perpetual adolescence. He thinks again of Bowersox's indictment of Jim Jolly on the radio, about how all the really talented people at the paper had long since moved on, and Carson is no longer angry. *How do I stay mad at the truth?*

Next come the questions Carson doesn't want to confront. Is this all some sort of cosmic payback for transgressions that lie further back? The way he disregarded his mother after his father passed, the unwillingness to hear Peter, the defiance that was not so much violent as it was abject disdain. What most people around Carson saw didn't change after Raymond died, at least not perceptibly. He remained a good enough student, a polite enough young man, a reliable enough friend. The fissures emerged in other ways. The cousins he'd grown up around, Peter's kids, hardly knew him. Peter's best advice would, invariably, send Carson in the opposite direction, even against his self-interest, as when Peter had an in at the University of Kentucky journalism school but Carson instead followed a lower-tier scholarship to Murray State. And although his mother had remained close to her boy by proxy through Raymond, Carson pulled away from those moorings after his father went into the ground. *Perhaps*, Carson thinks, *this is just the universe calling out my illusion of sovereignty. You like your life, pal? Well, watch this.* And then another thought shoves in: *What kind of man stands firm in his rejection of a God but is willing to cede everything to what the Buddhists call karma? A fucked-up man, for certain.*

Carson wraps his hand under Hector's jowls and works them like a stress ball, and Hector rumbles from deep inside his chest. The invocation of God, or whatever, brings fresh regret to the fore. Carson wishes he could talk to Cara now, about fear, about faith, about how to find the way up from the these depths. He wishes he hadn't torn out of Cincinnati, that he'd stayed and listened. He wishes he could go back to the apartment and answer that note. He figured he had time. He would even talk to Peter if he could.

The Ohio moves in streams and eddys, a gentle song in the deepening dark, and Carson at last gives himself over to sleep.

Carson awakens as if nudged. He cups his right hand on the back of his neck and massages the kinks. His head has been hanging like a broken flower. He has to pee, and from the smell, he gathers that Hector has already dropped a load nearby.

He puts a hand on his dog. "Come on, boy, let's go do some business."

Hector is cold, and though Carson knows, he scrambles onto his hands and knees and puts his face in front of his dog's, touching nose to nose. Hector's is dry. The hot breath Carson silently, futilely prays for does not come. He slips a hand over Hector's ribs and waits for the rise and fall of the lungs.

Nothing.

Carson pushes at the riverbank with his feet and slides in close, his arms and chest sinking into the urine and feces that Hector's played-out muscles released around him. He wraps his arms around his boy and he drops his face and head into Hector's fur, and he sobs for the best dog that ever was. He knows that Hector, an opportunistic dog, left when the leaving was still good, before Carson has to face what's coming.

"You could have said something," Carson says. "You could have told me you were going." He nestles his face into the dog's shoulder and breathes deep, a last whiff of his earthy companion.

Carson wishes against his manifest selfishness that Hector might have died at the home he knew, at the foot of the bed that belonged essentially to him, his dinner bowl and his box of chew toys in sight if he wanted one last look before he departed. *Was his last moment peaceful? Did he simply close his eyes and drift away, or was there terror that I could have eased if only I'd been awake?* Carson blinks, trying to banish the latter thought. He couldn't take that.

And then, at once, he's on another line of thought. Maybe the best version of Hector—certainly of Carson, but maybe Hector, too—lives in this cove, where they came so often when life seemed pregnant with possibility. Maybe Hector knew it, and knew his time had drawn near.

Carson hugs his dog and whispers into his ear. "I love you, boy."

Benny—

By the time you see this, my answer—the only one left to me—will be clear.

It's not that I think you're a bad guy, or even that I disagree with what you've decided to do. I just couldn't see my way to saying yes to you. I'll try to explain that.

You asked me to give you my heart, and that request told me that you don't get what I've been saying at all. I already gave you my heart, and you bruised it when you sold this place. You killed it for good when you bought it back and closed it. That was your right, of course, but I have rights, too. The right to not be a part of it. The right to do what I've done, no matter how dumb or self-destructive. You've obviously found a way to live with the consequences of your decisions. We'll see if I can live with mine.

If you're going to do this museum thing, my only plea to you is to do it right. I know you're proud of your daddy and your granddad, and that's all fine and good, but it was the people who came here every day who made this place what it was. Go get Jim Jolly and get him to run the newsroom displays. Nobody knows them better. Be sure to let people know what we did, the good things we did for this town. Our reporting, and the work of other papers around here, got bus laws changed after the Carrollton crash. Show that to people. Show them how we stood with them in depressions and recessions. Explain watchdog journalism, because I suspect that they won't appreciate our holding public officials to account until the next one tries to turn his office into a fiefdom (and he will, believe me).

The people who worked here loved this place—they loved it far longer than it loved them. Don't forget them, Benny.

That's what I have to say. That and good luck.

Carson

The Final Hours: 10:13 p.m.

Carson breaches the front door at Super Valu Saver a sniffling, shit-stained, teary mess. He thought he had cried himself out back at the river, but that was just the beginning. On the drive over, taking side streets and indirect angles to elude any patrolling cops, Carson looked when he could at Hector, half covered by a T-shirt in the front seat, and the collapses came in a devastating row, each one more debilitating than the last, until, finally, Carson reached the parking lot, found an unlit corner, and threw himself toward the door.

The ever-present security guard is turned the other way when Carson enters, a bit of serendipity. Carson makes a line for health and hygiene and slips into the aisles. He keeps his head low, trying to deny the ceiling cameras a good look even as he's sure, in his grief and mania, that they're all trained on him.

He crosses the big track that circles the store, a terse "excuse me" to the woman with the colicky baby whose cart he nearly walks into. A few steps more, and he's in the wilds of women's wear, in the tangled rows of lingerie and granny's underwear and ironically misspelled logo tees. He passes a girl who is checking out the fit of a bedazzle-bombed purple shirt. "It looks good," he says, out of breath, a breach in adult-to-teenage etiquette that brings an open-mouthed stare followed by a healthy roll of the eyes and then a scrunched-up face when his scent hits her. Carson keeps moving.

He veers left, through bath and shower, and emerges in lawn and garden, where he aimed to be. He considers the hanging line of shovels and homes in on the one sufficient for his sad duty, the pointed blade and long wooden handle well-suited for digging out ground on the riverbank. He pulls it down and heads for the front of the store.

Carson sticks to the main track now, the all-hours white light of the store assaulting his sleep-denied eyes. The place smells of ammonia and pine as the nighttime cleaning crew moves from station to station. Carson wonders if maybe this isn't some unsettling dream. This long walk to the checkstands is at once surreal and all too real, and discomfort and nausea chew at his guts.

He is alone at the front of the store. The checker and the security guard hear his approach, and they turn to him. In the next moment, their jaws drop away and Carson comes to a stop.

"Molly?"

MASH-unit Molly, his erstwhile and perpetually ill copy editor, nods and moves her mouth as if to speak, but she's swamped by the words of the guard moving up behind her.

"Sir, you'll need to put that down and come over here."

Carson backs up, dragging the blade of the shovel along the tile. The guard matches Carson's backward steps by moving forward. "I'm going to pay for this," Carson says. "I have to bury my dog."

"Put it down, sir."

"You don't understand."

The guard sets his hand on his holstered gun. The fingers quiver. "Sir, put it down and come here."

Carson backs up again, and again the guard closes the distance. "Look, man, I'll come back, but right now I have to bury my goddamned dog." The tears—*Jesus Christ, will they never end?*—spill from the inside corners of his eyes. He tastes them as the drainage runs to the corners of his mouth.

The guard steps forward and begins unsheathing his weapon, and Carson drops the shovel. It clangs against the tile floor.

Months later, during the hearing where Judge Tingley will approve the agreement stipulating seven years' imprisonment for Carson, with four years suspended, the genial old jurist will watch the video. He'll see Carson put his hands behind his head. He'll see the guard move up on Carson. He'll see Carson spin one-hundred-eighty degrees and send a sharp elbow crashing into the guard's face, felling him. He'll see Carson reach for the shovel and bolt toward the door, past Molly cowering in her checkstand. He'll see all of this, and he'll take off his glasses and rub the corners of his eyes.

"Mr. McCullough, two things about this case give me great pause," he'll say, the Muhlenberg County twang resonant in his learned words. "There's the incident with Mr. Bowersox, which you admitted to without prompting. And there's this one. When I see a violent man, Mr. McCullough, I see someone who has to prove to me that he can live among civilized people. You have friends and family members who say you can, and a life that up until April of this year seemed to say the same. But I want to hear it from you: Which man are you? The one on this tape, or the one in this courtroom?"

Carson will grip the lectern with perspiring hands and say, soft as the morning, "I'm the man who lost his way and is trying to get back. That's the general answer. The specific answer to this—" and he will wave a hand toward the stilled black-and-white courtroom monitor—"is that I just don't recognize this guy in myself. I'd lost my best friend, sir. If you're asking me if I'll ever do this again—no. No, I won't."

Judge Mason Tingley will consider that. He will consider that Carson has looked him in the eye, and Tingley will be just old-school enough to think that counts for something, and he'll say, "I'm going to try to have faith in you, son."

The Final Hours: 11:48 p.m.

Carson, knee-deep in a hole, rests his weight on the shovel handle. For a while there, his body churned out enough adrenaline to mask the pain in his side, but that minor consideration has passed. The duty has become labored, slow, and sheer agony. He has chosen this spot, up from the water line and under a big top of river birch, to leave Hector to the earth. Behind him is the rock where he took Cara down the first time, her hair splashed out around them, their lovemaking fierce and primal. Below sits the beach where young Hector learned to explore, his launching pad to attack the flat rocks that Carson would sidearm across the water. He was a good swimmer, a good boy, and Carson forces himself to get busy again so he can concentrate on something else.

He sets the blade and steps onto it, driving it deep into the rocky clay. Inches at a time, he expands the perimeter of the hole, until at last he's made a rectangle large enough to occupy Hector's body. The outline set, he digs between the new boundaries, extracting soil, until he reaches the depth he set earlier. He doesn't want to do this more than once. He uses the shovel handle to measure the depth, marking the spot with his finger, and then he carries the shovel around to the passenger side of the Mustang and measures that against his dog. *It'll do.*

Carson pitches the shovel onto the piles of riven clay. He squats like a baseball catcher and works his arms under Hector's body. The dog has grown stiff, and Carson is horrified by his relief at this development. A rigid body will be easier to lift and move, by the same principle that makes a box spring more cooperative than a mattress. The banality of this thought twists Carson's insides into a sailor's knot.

He lifts Hector up and out of the Mustang, his legs extending like pistons, his injured side aflame. He walks, unsteady, around the front of the car in the darkness, and the jagged footing threatens to send them both spilling to the ground. He moves forward, stepping with his left foot and dragging with his right, until his toes find the churned-up earth. The crying returns, drawn out by Hector's stench. Carson had always been proud that, whatever Hector's infirmities, he never became a smelly old dog. What Hector was able to fend off in life appears in death, however, and Carson thinks, not for the first time, that he's going crazy from the grief.

Carson falls to his knees and sets Hector down at the edge of his resting place. There's nothing to do now but bury him and get on with the rest of it. Carson pushes the pin on his watch that illuminates the digital face. It's 12:08 a.m. The attack at Super Valu Saver has surely sewn up the last of the details, and they'll be coming for him now.

He puts his hands on Hector's back, leans in and kisses the dog's ear, and rolls him into the grave. He pushes himself up, looks down upon Hector, and says, "You were my boy." The shovel finds purchase, and Carson returns the soil to where he found it.

When the job is done, the shovel is sent flying into the Ohio to be pulled along in the current to some other destiny. Carson settles into the driver's seat of the Mustang and turns the key. He'd put the top up to shield himself earlier, but there's no point in that now. It goes down. He disengages the parking brake and then sets the car into drive. He waggles his fingers on the steering wheel, ginning up his nerve, and then, fast so he can't back out, he lifts his foot from the brake and stomps on the accelerator, and the car rushes headlong into the river.

As it sinks away, headed for the bottom, Carson stretches himself out atop the water. The lazy lights of town blink before him, and he strokes his arms outward, builds up a bit of speed, and lets the current take over.

Dear Carson,

This will sound a bit counterintuitive, but bear with me. I think your grievances against God—or, to be true to what you said, the idea of God—are where a lot of people with some advanced education end up. I'm not saying that in the sense of educational elitism. I'm saying that the longer you've in the world, and the more you learn about the systems of man, the less you see room for God as he's generally imagined: as some kind of wizened old man in the sky who has boundless love for us and has us on some plan that seems incompatible with the way we destroy each other here on his Earth.

The Carrollton crash is an example of that. It's difficult to imagine how God could allow that to happen. It seems utterly incongruent with what he is portrayed as being. But consider this: Perhaps it's not a weakness in God, but in us, that we cannot see him against the backdrop of such a horrible event. When something like that strikes close to home—and for you, invades your every moment, home and work—we humans have a tendency to see it as the largest event in a very small world, when in fact it's a small event in a very large universe. (Please do not misunderstand that as diminishing those kids' deaths in any way. In our world, it was and is a massive tragedy. In the only world we can understand, it is devastating.)

When I find myself growing angry with God, and I do so more than you know, I try to remember that God is not for me to understand. A 17th-century Puritan clergyman, Stephen Charnock, put it like this: "God always is what he was, and always will be what he is." Viewed one way, that's hopelessly inscrutable, gibberish on the level of "it is what it is." But I take a different view, one of great comfort when I cannot explain the larger forces at work. God is constant. We—that is, fallible human beings—are the variables.

You did not ask for counsel, and I will not insult you by offering it. I will say, simply, that I draw comfort and grace from knowing, deep in my bones in a way that I cannot prove empirically (as you noted), that God is with us and abides, even when we cannot. This isn't about going to church, Carson, or engaging in the ceremony. It's about finding and honoring that peace with your maker. It's about being OK in the knowledge that there's something bigger and more powerful than we are. In other words, life is hard enough. No need to seek out burdens you weren't meant to carry.

Your old boss, Benny Haller, held a sneak preview of his museum, and Ruby and I went to check it out. He asked how you were, and we told him you're doing fine. We went through the exhibits and saw so much of your fine work, and I want you to know that we're proud of you. Then and now. Your Mom and Dad would be proud, too.

Your Aunt Ruby has been battling a cold the past few days, so I've been doing the cooking. Hot dogs and frozen waffles are growing tedious around here, so I hope she rallies soon. I've reduced my constitutional to three days a week instead of five. It had begun to tax me a bit too much. We're getting old, Carson. It happens. Enjoy your youth while you still have it. Everything's relative.

I'll let you go now. We'll be along in a few weeks to check in on you.

Uncle Peter

The Final Hours: 12:34 a.m.

The free-flowing river ride ends downtown, under the Maxine Brockbirch Bridge. Carson, a bad athlete in most things but always a strong swimmer, angles against the flow toward the embankment. He crawls onto the concrete pad and sits at the water's edge. His shoes come off, and then the socks. He wrings them out. He pulls the T-shirt over his head and squeezes the water from that, too. All that the Ohio River is finds its way to Carson's nose. Fish feces (human shit, too), river weeds, industrial chemicals, arsenic, chromium, motor oil—it's all in there, and more, and it batters Carson's nose and eyes.

Carson dresses quickly and then crab-crawls to the street level on Donerail Avenue. The downtown streets are lonely, but Carson knows there is peril. He'll have to make two major crossings, here and at Julep Street, and that means passing under street lamps, in view of open windows and, perhaps, the eyes hidden behind them. Or maybe it will be a city cop, his cruiser parked and darkened in some alley, who spots him on the move and takes him down.

Carson silently counts to ten, the heaving of his chest marking each beat. His side aches, and he has so much more to demand of it yet. At ten, he walks. The pace is ragged and unstable as he fights against fear to move at a normal gait. His mind tells him with all rationality that he'll be less auspicious this way. His heart, forcing its way up, implores him to run.

On the other side, he slips into the alley between First National and Johansen Pawn, and he presses his back against the red brick. His heart plays a rock anthem in his chest, all bombast and beat. His mouth is dry, and his nose smells terror. He tries to slow his breathing. He thinks of halcyon days and of his parents, a time when only little-boy concerns crowded into his world. *Thank God they didn't see this.* At last, when he's ready, he walks again, steadier, to the next alley.

It goes like this for ten blocks, a stair-stepping up and over as Carson makes his way to Julep Street. On the edge of downtown, he comes up against a cragged man in threadbare layers, pushing a Super Valu Saver cart brimming with discovered treasures. They approach each other casually, as if two chums crossing paths at a cocktail party.

"D'you have any change, sire?" The filth and the alcohol trailing of the bum's breath form a noxious brew, and Carson edges away.

"No, I don't." He puts his head down and moves along.

"Well, you don't have to be nasty about it, sire."

Faster now.

The old man dumps his cart and begins kicking his belongings through the alley, raging against the judgments of surly interlopers and the whisperings in his own head. Carson breaks into a dead run. He crosses the boundary line where the vagrant downtown buildings fall back and the old-money neighborhoods begin. Two blocks up, on drowsy Julep Street, the empty husk of the *Argus-Dispatch* building rises from the corner. Benny Haller, it seems, has extinguished the exterior lights in a cost-cutting move. *Oh, lucky day.*

A police cruiser slides by on Julep Street, headed downtown, and Carson steps back into the shadows. Disturbance call, probably. An alley two blocks back, in all likelihood.

Carson needs no better reason. He heads for the street.

He breaches the building from the backside, next to the abandoned delivery bays. The all-purpose key Benny told him to keep a week ago still works, and Carson steps into the newsprint storage room. It smells of fresh-cut lumber and pulp. Carson, cast in darkness as the door closes behind him, runs searching hands on the inside wall, like a teenager feeling up his first date, until he finds the switch. The fluorescents flicker on.

The place sits empty, save for the newsprint leavings that swirl around the floor in the drafty air. A week ago, when the *Argus-Dispatch* was yet a going concern, the cavernous holding area was full, a terrain of cheap-paper mountains. But Benny Haller is no fool. Newsprint has been fetching $650 per metric ton, and when he bought the *Argus-Dispatch* he inherited many such tons. The thought of all that paper going down the road to St. Louis or Cincinnati—wherever Haller might find a deal and someone willing to move the goods—reminds Carson of the calculations he had to make a few years ago, when the staff cuts became less anomalies and more quarterly rote. He would get a revised budget from the Mantooth mothership in Paducah, one that reflected not only whatever shortfalls his own paper was experiencing but also the collective financial grief of the company, and then he would consider the width of his options. In the newspaper game, a manager who wishes to manipulate the books has three places to look: raw materials (paper and ink), operational funds (*memo to staff: please stop taking pencils home with you*), and labor (that is, people). Carson remembers the days of the first few budgetary directives, when he would dance around his living room after saving a couple of reporters by tightening the page counts, closing an open position, and moving some travel money around. He also remembers the many cuts that came later, when no amount of creative arithmetic and budgetary gymnastics could blunt his sad duty. When people started walking out of this place with corrugated boxes holding their professional identities, under the watch of security guards and with their former colleagues trying not to look, that's when Carson began to hate the job.

And now, if he could, he would kick his own ass right here, for just bending over and taking it again and again. *Why didn't you quit, chickenshit? Why didn't you save some of them?*

It's a pointless question, because he knows the answer too well: *Nobody was going to be saved. Not here.*

The next door leads to more of the same, the familiar and the unfamiliar in a static stalemate. The press, a three-unit Goss offset, has been dismantled. Its contents lie in a score of pine boxes heaped along the wall, under the portal windows where Carson and the others watched the last edition roll. Decades' worth of grime outlines where the units sat, the concrete underneath them seeing light for the first time since it was poured. It puts Carson in a mind of a story old Burton Haller liked to tell at the company Christmas party, after he'd slid a few cocktails down his throat and lost his natural inhibitions around the help. When Bertram Haller merged his beloved *Argus* with the *Dispatch* in '33, the first thing he did was dismantle his own letterpress and bury it in a half-dozen graves in deepest Hancock County and replace it with the nicer unit the *Dispatch* was using. It was the act not of a man with a poor business acumen but one with a highly developed sense of pragmatism. It eliminated the possibility that anyone could come to town and turn that piece of machinery against him and his newly hyphenated kingdom. So it was that in Benny Haller's own way, he was doing the same thing. Encased in a museum display, this artifact of twentieth-century communication will never turn again, never set down another word. It will go on in stasis, a silent testament to the way things used to be.

In the newsroom, the surreal reveal is complete. Cubicles have been dismantled and stacked in fours. Someone has written "school district" in black Sharpie on a piece of printer paper and taped it to one of the stacks. Office chairs graze in a far corner, as if rounded up by sheep hounds. Fifteen years' worth of computer monitors—recent flat screens and relics of the last century that look like cannon ordnance—are stacked on pallets. Hard drives and keyboards lie on another pallet. The drives have been wiped down, the software to resuscitate them packed neatly into sandwich bags and taped to their hard plastic bodies.

Carson makes a quick lap around the newspaper offices, and it's the same everywhere. Equipment is bundled up, stacked, separated, and processed to move.

He has come here with intent, not a mind for nostalgia. The *Argus-Dispatch* won three Kentucky Better Newspaper sweepstakes under his watch, a few regional Society of Professional Journalists baubles and sundry staff writing awards, all of which graced a wall in the foyer. *Fuck Benny Haller if he thinks he's taking that stuff.* Carson's legacy isn't going to be put behind glass. He'll get it out of here and someplace safe, someplace he can get to after the unpleasantness he has unleashed runs its course.

And there's the matter of the record. Microfiche. Carson walked in this place on May 26, 1986, and got pushed out on an

April day twenty-six years later, and those editions are his more than they are anybody else's who gives a damn. It's his life's best work, the proof that was he was here and he mattered, and that's precious to him now that everyone else seems so willing to forget. The only thing he loved more sits in a fresh clay grave a mile and a half upriver. He's taking this, and that's all there is to it.

Carson finds a packing box propped against the wall of his empty office. He folds it into usefulness and tapes it up, and then he sets it in the middle of the room. He scurries off to begin gathering the items he is intent on annexing. The air inside the room hangs heavy and acrid, as if the ghostly vapors of every cigarette and every cup of coffee have come down from the ceiling and the darkest corners of the place like stalking cats to see what happens next.

The Final Hours: 1:51 a.m.

The folly of irrational thinking hits Carson as he does inventory. Before him, in the middle of the newsroom he once led, sits everything he came for: three-hundred and eight boxed rolls of microfiche—May 1986 to December 2011. The final four months of his dreary parade haven't been transferred yet. The hard-copy editions sit in page-size binders marked January, February, March, April. These recent pages torture him. The ones encased in film are transferrals, replicas of what once was. But these pages, so recent that Carson can still smell the ink on them, speak to the *Argus-Dispatch*'s maddening inconsistency in its final days. Failure became rampant (Carson, in briefly thumbing through some of the clips, found eight misspellings), but on the right night his staff could still deliver, as it did with the Wildcats' just-completed run to the NCAA championship. Carson runs a finger along the spine of a binder and moves on. Fifty-seven pieces of award hardware—trophies and plaques and certificates behind glass—fill three large moving boxes. The microfiche fill another three. The binders sit atop them. And Carson's car lies at the bottom of the Ohio River.

He considers the obvious options and summarily dismisses each. A summoned cab will bring attention here before Carson wants it, and he still harbors hope of eluding imminent capture. Hucking these things one at a time is both impractical—*where to hide them?*—and time-consuming. His action, whatever it is, has to be done before morning light. Two forklifts sit idle in the empty newsprint room and could easily carry this out, but once he's on the street...*yeah, that's absurd.*

Carson remembers seeing a flatbed dolly where the ad sales team used to sit. That will make an easier go of it. Maybe he can load it up and wheel it out of here and give himself a chance, at least. He breaks into a jog—expediency outweighing the pain—and when he sees the face staring back at him through the glass in the double doors, it's all Carson can do to remain upright and breathing.

Red Strummer raps at the glass with a freckled, filthy hand. "Open up."

Carson, unsteady still, speaks to him through the glass. "What do you want?"

"What are you doing here, Carson?"

"What are you doing here, Red?"

Red, fifty-something with crumpled ginger skin that hangs loose around his neck, pushes a piece of paper against the glass. "Got a letter from Benny Haller. He's closing the place."

"Yeah, well, no biggie. You can repair engines somewhere else."

"What are you doing?" Red asks.

"Taking some stuff that belongs to me. You know how that is, right? Seems that you've taken some stuff that belongs to me, too. A couple of workstations, maybe?"

Red's laugh is expectorant, wheezy, a two-packs-of-Camelunfiltered-a-day rasp that fogs the glass. "I'm offended."

"No, you're not."

"Come on, Carson, open up."

Carson reaches for the drawstring to close the blinds. "Sorry, Red. We're closed."

The Final Hours: 3:33 a.m.

Carson stands shivering on the north end of the bridge, his city in a fraying dark behind him, Indiana dead ahead. He looks back and then forward, and then he slumps against the trussing, the April clip book and his 1989 Kentucky Journalist of the Year trophy dropping to the asphalt beside him. The gold-painted plastic figurine head on the trophy snaps off and rolls away from him. His arms pulsate from the effort of carrying the items, and Carson deep-rubs his bicep.

He's out of ideas. More than that, he's out of will. And here he is, stuck in between.

He laughs. It comes out maniacal, and then it crumbles, and Carson drops his head onto his arm and he gives in to the sobs. The regrets come again, all of them. Cara, Dan, Timmy. His father. His mother. Peter. Peter, especially, among the living. Hector. *Oh, God, Hector.* And then, without segue, he's thinking of Jagur, wondering if the highway man finally found his way back. Crazy-ass Jagur makes perfect sense now. Home slips away from us if we're not careful. It goes not all at once, but in increments often too small to measure. It's lost in the calculus of minor disregard and misdemeanors of the heart, of good intentions and poor follow-through, and by the time we notice it's getting away from us, it might as well be gone. Jagur had the gumption to do something about it. Carson thinks, too, of the old bum patrolling the alleys. By the time Carson had come back through, having left most of his treasures behind, the previous insult had been forgotten and the old guy accepted Carson's offer of the *Argus-Dispatch* petty-cash jar with appropriate cheer. "I'll be raising a toast to you, sire."

Carson lifts his filling eyes southward to Julep Street. The other side of the world now.

A honk brings Carson hurtling out of the folds of sleep. Directly in front of him, Lurleen's bosom bubbles over the top of her pickup door.

"You going where I'm going?" she asks.

Carson pushes himself into a squat and then stands, slowly. His hamstrings feel like brittle rubber bands, ready to snap. The wind has cut through his wet clothes, and his teeth chatter.

"Got a cellphone?" he asks her.

"Why?"

"I'm supposed to meet someone here."

She passes the phone to him. "You're chilled to the bone," she says as his hand brushes hers in taking it.

He flips the phone open and punches in the number. He holds it to his ear. "It's not ringing."

"You gotta hit 'send,' hon."

Carson listens again. "Yeah, this is Carson McCullough. I'm on the north end of the Brockbirch Bridge. No, I'm not. Just me. Yeah. I understand. No problem."

He drops his hand from his ear to his hip.

"They coming?"

"Yeah."

"You gotta hit 'end.'"

"I will. Just a second."

"I can't just idle here on the bridge," she says.

He doesn't look at her. "You're OK. Nobody's here but us."

Carson keeps his eyes on the town. The first white car turns right on Julep Street, blue strobe engaged. Then comes another. A third. A fourth. The line of blue spinning lights moves northward, homing in. Two blocks behind them, a Subaru turns left onto Julep Street and gives chase to the chasers.

I'll be damned, Carson thinks. *That scanner-following fool.*

"Why are you smiling?" Lurleen says. "Is it some delicious secret, darling?"

Carson closes the phone and hands it to her. "Thanks for the help." He pats his shirt pocket. Cara's words, surely worse for the swim, are still with him. He stoops for his papers and his trophy, and he starts walking south on the footpath.

"I'm sorry about that night," she calls after him. "Your eye looks better."

Carson turns and faces her. "Don't be. I deserved it."

"Sure you don't want a ride, honey?"

He waves her off. "I'm sure. Take care of yourself, Lurleen. I'll be seeing you."

She bites down on a loose syllable and starts the pickup. He's twenty yards away now. He doesn't turn back.

The cruisers mount the far side of the bridge and bear down. Carson keeps moving. One foot, then the other. There will be no struggle. Only acceptance and submission. He's ready. Now, finally, he wants what's coming.

The cars stop, three-wide on the bridge. Cops squat behind open doors, service revolvers drawn. Carson, so tired, moves forward. One foot, then the other.

He sees Peter breach the front of the police line. An officer intercepts him, slipping a massive arm around Peter's chest and walking him back as the old man flails.

Carson stops. The cops are fifty feet ahead of him now, barking directions that dissipate in the air. He drops his items for the last time and follows them to his knees. Fingers entwine behind his head. His elbows run parallel to the water below.

The strobe lights slide across the bridge and the downtown buildings. Blue uniforms fly at Carson, and he looks right through them, to something beyond. Something he's seeing for the first time. His city has never been so beautiful as this.

He closes his eyes. The first body crashes into Carson's, taking him to the asphalt.

It's OK now.

I'm home.

Dan ...

Getting out tomorrow. I want to thank you for the letter of support to the parole board. It was a great, unexpected surprise.

I know I've already apologized to you about that stuff a few years ago, but I want to tell you again how sorry I am, and how foreign that all seems to me now. A lot of people stayed in my corner when I didn't deserve it, but I think outside of Benny you did most of all.

I'm going home. My aunt and uncle kept up the tax payments on my folks' house, and I'm going to move back there, into my old bedroom, while I try to get my feet under me. My Uncle Peter died last year, so being there will let me keep tabs on Aunt Ruby. My PO's letting me do my community service through Peter and Ruby's church. Landscaping and whatnot. Food drives. Litter pickup. There are folks there who've been good to me while I've been in, and I appreciate that very much. One of the last things Peter asked of me before he died was if I'd think about being baptized. Funny old guy. We talked a lot about some really deep stuff the past few years, and I finally found out that he wasn't the rigid old Bible-thumper I always believed him to be. I guess he just wants to hedge his bets with the better version of me. Now that I'm getting out, I think I'm going to do it. I can't say that I'm ready to believe, but I have an open mind. One thing I know: I'm going to have to live different from how I lived before. So maybe this can be part of that. I can't recommend much about the prison experience except this: There's clarity to be had, if you're willing to receive it.

I heard about the Times closing. I'm really sorry, man. It was inevitable, I guess, but it's still hard. It's not the same world you and I graduated into, is it?

Well, that's it, I guess. I'd say I'll see you soon, but who knows when that will be. I have a lot of work to do. But I didn't want to let the opportunity pass to tell you how much I appreciate what you did for me. I'm not going to let you down.

Your old bud,

Carson

P.S. Forgot to tell you where I'll be working. My PO got me a job as a line cook at Shoney's, which is a good enough place to start, I guess.

The first job he pitched me on was as a night stocker at Super Valu Saver. Can you believe that?

Acknowledgments

This novel sat in a digital folder on my computer for three years, waiting patiently for me to re-read it and see my way to the finish. So I guess I'll start by thanking time. It has a way of bringing clarity, if you're willing to sit still long enough to receive it.

Most of my work is built on the foundation—or, perhaps, the folly—of time spent in my own head. This one required more in the way of conversations that pushed the boundaries of what I believe and/or am willing to consider. For that, I appreciate the Rev. Aaron Householder and Dr. Stephen Benoit, two people I've known clear back to high school (and in Benoit's case, far longer than that). Thanks for making me stretch.

Jim Thomsen is a reliable friend and deft editor. I'm grateful.

I spent twenty-five years in the newspaper game, and a lot of that time is distilled here. Twenty-three years were mostly enjoyable; the final two seemed endless and a bit cruel. That attitude no doubt spilled over into this work. At the very least, I've tried to be fair.

I've got a hell of a family, the one I was born to and the one that welcomed me into the fold more recently. The Clineses and Lancasters and Lorellos and Mottolas—you're the best. I mean it.

Cass, Dina, Bob, Jon, Laura, John, Barbara, Huckleberry, Jennifer, Linda, Wayne—love to you all.

In my 23rd and 24th years, I spent about eighteen months working at a newspaper in western Kentucky, in a town not unlike the unnamed, fictitious place that anchors this story. I was fortunate enough to work with a bunch of folks right around my age, mostly single, mostly up for good times. We packed a lot into our time together, and as I've gotten older I've also become progressively appreciative of how fortunate I was for that experience. So to Heen and Lovett, Biv and Cindy, the Toddler and Newton, Hunter and Ben and Noelle: thank you ever so much for those seasons in my life.

And, finally, there's Elisa. Always, always Elisa. Baby, let's keep going.

About the Author

Craig Lancaster is the author of such novels as *600 Hours of Edward* and *Edward Adrift*, and a frequent contributor to magazines and newspapers as a writer and an editor.

600 Hours of Edward, his debut, was a Montana Honor Book and the 2010 High Plains Book Award winner for best first book. His work has also been honored by the Utah Book Awards (the novel *The Summer Son*) and with an Independent Publisher Book Awards gold medal (the short-story collection *The Art of Departure*), among other citations.

Before writing fiction, he worked at newspapers big and small in Texas, Alaska, Ohio, California, Washington, Montana and, yes, Kentucky. He's never crossed the Maxine Brockbirch Bridge (it's fictional), but he knows that stretch of the Ohio

River well from another time and place. Long may it roll.

Lancaster lives in Billings, Montana, with his wife, bestselling author Elisa Lorello (*Faking It, Pasta Wars, The Second First Time*).

ALSO BY CRAIG LANCASTER

600 Hours of Edward
The Summer Son
The Art of Departure
Edward Adrift
The Fallow Season of Hugo Hunter
This Is What I Want
Edward Unspooled

CONNECT WITH CRAIG

On the Web: www.craig-lancaster.com
Twitter: @AuthorLancaster
Facebook: www.facebook.com/authorcraiglancaster